# MURDER IN THE ROUND

*A Pamela Barnes Acoustic Mystery*

by

Patricia Rockwell

For information, email **Cozy Cat Press**, cozycatpress@aol.com or visit our website at: www.cozycatpress.com

COZY CAT
PRESS

ISBN: 978-0-9881943-3-5
Printed in the United States of America

Cover design by Scott Saunders of *Design 7 Studio*
www.design7studio.com

1 2 3 4 5 6 7 8 9 10

This book is dedicated to all my friends in community theater—especially Cité des Arts in Lafayette, Louisiana, and Abbey Players in Abbeville, Louisiana. Some of the best moments in my life have occurred on stage.

## CHAPTER 1

"Why did I ever let you drag me here, Pamela?" whispered Rocky Barnes out of the corner of his mouth, a fake smile plastered on his face. He squirmed uncomfortably in the red velvet seat, being cautious not to rub his arm against the rather rotund older gentleman seated to his right.

"Shh, Rocky," replied his wife with the same polite smile and soft voice. She nudged him surreptitiously with her right elbow. "You'll love this play. It's a famous piece of British literature, for heaven's sake. You're an English teacher. If anyone should appreciate it, it should be you!" She leaned in front of her husband and proffered her benign smile to the older gentleman on her husband's right who had glanced at them.

Rocky gave a muffled snort and chewed on his lower lip as he hunkered down in his seat.

"I hate this seating arrangement," he whispered. "I feel like I'm the one on stage. The audience members over there all seem to be looking at me." He nodded toward the open stage area to the other side of the little acting area. "It's like seeing a show in a bull fighting ring." Instead of bullfighters, however, latecomers were still looking for their seats, crossing right across the stage with compunction. The seated audience members paid no attention to them and continued their pre-show conversations.

"Oh, good Lord!" Pamela said, closer to his face now. "It's just theater in the round. We're lucky we got seats in the front row."

"You're lucky," he said. "I'm feeling exposed. Why couldn't we sit further back?"

"Because Joan got us these seats," explained Pamela. "Front row seats, I might add. One of the benefits of my best friend having a lead role." She puffed out her chest proudly.

"Your friend Joan is always up to some new escapade," he continued. Pamela could envision imaginary steam pouring from his nostrils. "I think she's the one who's always egging you on . . ."

"Egging me on?" exclaimed Pamela in whispered horror. "Really, Rocky!" She crossed her arms and legs in dramatic punctuation of her annoyance.

"Sorry," he said quickly. "Normally I enjoy outings with you, but I feel like I'm on display in this place."

"It's not my fault that Arliss's baby is home sick with the croup!" she said. "Believe me, I'd much prefer her company. At least I know she'd be supportive of Joan and her dramatic debut."

"That croup story sounds fishy to me," added Rocky. "Probably just a ploy Arliss is using to get out of sitting through some amateur production of 'The Importance of Being Earnest.' Oh, well. I'm here so I guess I'll make the best of it." He shrugged and sighed, placing his elbows on the arm rests and crossing one large leg over the other defiantly. Pamela ignored him as she grabbed her oversized pocketbook from the floor under her chair and began rummaging around in it. "What are you looking for?"

"This," she said as she removed a small audio recorder. "I promised Arliss I'd record the show for her. So, even though she can't be here, she'll be able to hear Joan's performance." She pushed some buttons and set the volume control device.

"Why didn't you just bring our camcorder?" he asked. "You could get a video of it?"

"Oh, Rocky," she scowled. "I can't do that! First of all, I certainly couldn't enjoy the show if I had to watch it through the viewfinder of a camcorder, but more important, the theater won't allow anyone to video record a performance—or take photographs. It says so right in the program if you'd bothered to read it." Rocky grabbed the theater program from the floor where he'd placed it after glancing at it perfunctorily when they'd first arrived. He skimmed through the few pages and found the statement in small print indicating exactly what Pamela had just said.

"I don't think an audio recording will be that exciting for your friend," he said.

"It's better than nothing," she added. "Hopefully, the show will run for weeks and Arliss will be able to come and see a regular performance when Noah gets better. Until then, I'm doing my part to make both of my friends happy. I'm setting the speed for 'slow' so the recorder will run for at least four hours. That should cover the length of the performance." She completed the settings on the audio recorder and when she was assured that it was running properly, she placed it in a side pocket of her purse where the microphone would be positioned to face the stage in front of her.

"I don't know how that Joan has time for all of this acting stuff and her job too," he huffed. "Every time I turn around, she's up to some new scheme." He was still thumbing through the brightly printed program that listed the cast of characters, complete with each actor's photograph.

"Acting in a community theater production is hardly a scheme, Rocky," noted Pamela. "Joan is very civic minded. She's on the theater board and has always been a strong supporter of the arts. And, of course, she's anxious for the theater's new venue here above the Reardon Coffee Factory to be successful. She's taken a personal interest in it. As has James."

Pamela was aware that Rocky knew all about her friend Joan Bentley. She and Joan were colleagues in the Psychology Department as well as close personal friends. Joan had supported Pamela on numerous detecting adventures of hers in the past and Pamela had allowed herself to become embroiled in many of Joan's antics too. At least, that's how Rocky seemed to view it. He'd realized that Pamela perceived him as overprotective and had tried to tone down his worrying. In truth, he and Pamela functioned much better when he treated her as an equal—which, of course, she was.

The 'James' she'd mentioned was James Grant, Reardon's brand new mayor and a close personal friend of Joan's. Pamela and Joan had been instrumental in assisting him in his recent successful bid for mayor—even helping exonerate him from being charged in his wife's murder. Now, the new mayor was living up to expectations by pushing to revive the town's community theater company. He had spearheaded the effort to find the theater company a new home upstairs over a local landmark—the Reardon Coffee Factory.

The Factory sat in the center of the central downtown square. It was built over the remains of

Romulus Reardon's original coffee factory—the very place that had put Reardon on the map during the Civil War. Back then, the Reardon Coffee Factory had produced alternative coffee from various local plants when the Confederacy was unable to secure coffee beans due to Union blockades. Today, 'the Factory' served sandwiches, salads, and an array of coffee substitute beverages. It was well known worldwide and visitors came from around the globe to sample its unusual 'coffee' drinks. Thanks to the town's new mayor, James Grant, and a host of other civic-minded individuals, customers could now not only dine at the Factory; they could also go upstairs and enjoy a theatrical production.

"Has Joan ever acted before?" Rocky asked casually as he perused the program.

"I don't think so," replied Pamela. "She may have. She certainly doesn't seem nervous. But then, you know Joan. There's not much that frightens her. I'm sure she'll be marvelous as...Lady Bracknell." She double-checked the name of Joan's character and then took a deep breath, delighted that their pre-show conversation had turned to more innocuous topics. An irate Rocky was difficult enough to handle at home, but much worse to deal with in public. She'd rather discuss the history of Joan's acting career with him.

"Doesn't look like they have much scenery," noted Rocky, now glancing around at the small, circular stage before them.

"How much can they have?" asked Pamela. "I mean, if they put up walls or something tall, the people across from us won't be able to see." She was right. The stage was labeled 'theater-in-the-round' and, in truth, the acting area was totally round. The audience, seated on all sides of the circular stage, was arranged in bleachers of four tiers.  There were four entrances and exits placed like cuts in a pie at the one-fourth positions.  On the floor-level stage, the scenery was minimal as Rocky had noted.  A blue-flowered love seat, a white lacquered desk with matching chair, a small wicker table and two chairs, and a white bench were the only items of furniture—all placed in various locations on the stage floor.

"Do you know anyone else in the cast?" Rocky asked her as he perused the list of characters.

"A few," she replied, glancing at her own program. "There's one fellow who's a local lawyer.  I think I remember Joan mentioning him.  Another guy is retired, maybe from the Police Department, I think.  Oh, and this fellow is a computer programmer with that new manufacturing company that just opened." She pointed at one of the male characters.

"It appears the only cast members you know are the male ones," said Rocky, turning to her with a frown.

"That's because they're the only ones whom Joan talks about, Rocky!" she said, pouting.  "It's not like I know any of these people personally.  It's a small cast. I've heard Joan talk about some of her cast mates but I haven't met any of them."

At that moment, the house lights began to dim.

"Oh, I think they're ready to start," whispered Pamela.  She reached down and adjusted her purse, making certain her audio recorder was functioning.

"Is your recorder working?" Rocky asked her quickly.

"Yes, yes," she replied.  "I set it and it's been recording you for the last few minutes.  It'll pick up the show just fine."

"Ugh," he moaned as he closed his program and leaned back to concentrate on the performance. "You'll probably use my words to blackmail me."

"You mean all those nasty things you said about my friends?" she asked with a sly smile.

Rocky mumbled but otherwise remained silent only because the lights were lowering and the entire audience were concluding their own personal conversations and becoming quiet. After the total blackout, Pamela could hear actors entering quietly from the entrance ways. When the lights came up on the central stage area, two men dressed in Edwardian finery began a dialogue that immediately indicated their relationship as gentleman and butler. Pamela was soon engaged in the play and her recent discussion with her husband seemed far away. Shortly into the play, Joan Bentley made her entrance as Lady Bracknell, the mother of the show's heroine. Joan's character was larger than life, overbearing, authoritarian, and brilliant—much like Joan herself. Of course, Joan was nowhere near as pushy as Lady Bracknell, thought Pamela, but Joan and her character did share a devastating wit. As the play progressed, Pamela enjoyed listening to Joan's lines and comparing her friend to this fictional character. Joan made a marvelous Lady Bracknell, she realized. That her friend was a wonderful actress did not come as a complete surprise to Pamela, but it was still a thrill to see Joan flaunt her talents here in this public arena—even if it was only a community production.

Soon, the first scene in the first act ended in a blackout. Pamela could hear actors and stagehands moving about quickly—actors apparently exiting and stagehands making small changes to the scenery and props on stage.  At least, she surmised that's what was happening, as she couldn't really see anything in the dark.  After a brief few minutes, the stage lights came back up, and the next scene began.  In this scene, Joan was seated almost in front of Pamela at the small table with the actress who was playing her daughter, Gwendolyn.  Pamela enjoyed the delightful dialogue between the two actresses as they held and drank from cups of a delicate rose-covered china tea set.

The actress portraying Gwendolyn said a line and then daintily sipped tea from her cup while awaiting her stage mother's response.  As Joan delivered a delightful monologue, the young actress across the table from her appeared to choke.  Joan looked up briefly at her acting partner, but continued her speech. When Joan's speech ended and it was obvious that it was the younger woman's turn to speak, the young actress grabbed her throat and gasped audibly, attempting to speak without success.  Joan reached over and patted "Gwendolyn" on her back gently. Pamela had no idea whether this stage business was planned or if it was spontaneous, but she was absolutely certain that the next event was not in Oscar Wilde's original script.

Gwendolyn rose, still clutching her throat tightly, and reached out with her free hand, trying to speak. As the entire audience watched in horror, the young actress suddenly fell to the stage floor.

## CHAPTER 2

A woman screamed and suddenly the audience was all atwitter.  A tall man strode through one of the aisle entrances and rushed to the fallen woman. A man and a woman who had been sitting in the front row across the stage floor from Pamela also rushed onstage and both bent down beside the actress on the floor.  The tall man bent low and tried to revive the young woman.   Then he looked up and scanned his eyes around the audience and asked if there was a physician present.  A man in the second row in Pamela's section of the house rose quickly and headed onto the stage towards the woman.  He bent over her and listened and immediately began to perform CPR.  The tall man pulled a cell phone from his pocket and apparently called 911.  The entire audience gasped.

"What's wrong?" asked Rocky.  "This isn't part of the show, is it?"

"I don't think so," replied Pamela. "I don't know the play.  Does this character collapse?  Do you know?"

"I don't think so," said Rocky.  "I can't remember, but surely even if she did, they wouldn't call someone from the audience to tend to her."

"Maybe it's audience participation," suggested Pamela.

They both watched the doctor administer to the woman on the floor as the tall man who now stood in the center of the stage watched.   Eventually, the doctor stopped his ministrations, looked up at the man, and sadly shook his head. The woman on the floor beside the actress cried and the young man next to her clutched the prone actress to his chest.

"I'm so sorry, everyone," said the tall man to the audience, making a feeble attempt to cover the scene with his body. "I'm Ron Whitcomb, the director. We're cancelling tonight's performance due to the...illness of one of our actresses." Appearing uncomfortable, he looked behind him at the woman on the floor and the doctor beside her. "Please retain your ticket stubs from tonight's performance and we will honor them if...when...we reschedule tonight's show. Thank you so much for coming to the Reardon Community Theater's first performance in our new home and we promise we will do our best to reschedule as soon as we can. Thank you." He smiled pathetically around at the audience and made a vague gesture for them to leave. Slowly as if in a daze, the members of the audience began to exit the small theater.

Rocky ushered Pamela carefully out the aisle they had originally entered, following the slow-moving crowd, all muttering in whispered tones. They all traipsed down the wooden stairs to the main floor of the Coffee Factory. It seemed as if everyone was moving in zombie-like precision until they had completely escaped the scene of what had appeared to be a sudden death.

Only when the couple was inside their car did either of them venture any comment.

"What do you think happened?" asked Rocky, leaning back behind the wheel. Making no attempt to start the engine, he looked over at Pamela.

"I have no idea," she responded.  "I mean, that man, the director I guess, tried to put a polite spin on it, but it was obvious that the doctor's efforts were not successful.  That woman died, Rocky."  She swallowed noticeably.

"I wonder if she'd been ill," he offered.  "She looked healthy."

"You can't always tell," said Pamela.

"Did Joan ever discuss her?" he asked.

"I don't remember," replied his wife.  "She may have, but mostly she talked about the men in the production, as I told you.  You know Joan."

"Surely she knows something about this young woman.  I mean, she played her mother."  Rocky sighed and started the engine.  They pulled out of their parallel spot on the darkened downtown side street and headed towards home.

Pamela was thinking.  She mumbled some answer to Rocky, but her mind kept replaying the scene of the young woman's collapse and apparent death on the spot. How horrible!  It was bad enough to have been sitting so close to this terrible tragedy as it occurred, but Joan, who surely knew this woman at least somewhat, must be mortified.  What must she be going through right now?  Pamela agonized about what to do.  Should she call Joan?  What would be the best thing to do to help her friend?  She didn't want to bother her if she was involved in dealing with the aftermath of the young actress's death, but then again, she didn't want Joan to think that she had just deserted her.  Joan had known she'd been there in the audience.  Would she have expected Pamela and Rocky to remain behind to comfort her?

"Maybe we should have stayed," suggested Pamela.

"They told us to leave," replied Rocky, slowing his foot on the gas. "What makes you say that?"

"What if Joan needs me?" she asked. "This will surely be a huge shock to her."

"Not if what you've told me is correct," he said. "You said she only seemed interested in the men in the cast."

"But that woman died right on the floor in front of her. Should I call her?" asked Pamela.

"No," said Rocky. "She has your number. Lord knows, she's not shy about calling you if she needs something. She's done it often enough."

"We're friends," said Pamela. "She's done plenty of supportive things for me."

"I know," he said. "Pam, your friend Joan is—if nothing else—capable of taking care of herself. If she needs to speak to you, she'll call. I don't think you need to hang on her like a mother hen in this situation."

"You're right," she agreed. "I'm just trying to be pro-active. It's a normal reaction when there's really nothing you can do. And what can I do? A young woman is dead." She let the statement hang in the air.

"You're sure she's dead?" he asked.

"Rocky!" she cried. "They called a doctor out of the audience. He performed CPR. Didn't you see that? He tried everything possible to revive the woman, but he wasn't successful. I think they called an ambulance too, but, as it was, there didn't appear to be any need to do that."

"Yeah, very sad," he agreed. "It's hard to believe that anyone who appeared that lively and healthy could just die so suddenly."

"I know," she said. "Maybe she had some congenital heart defect. Or something like that. You hear stories of people just collapsing and dying while they're running in marathons and they find out after the autopsy that they had some major heart problem or something."

"Possibly," he said, nodding slowly. "She seemed fine until she started drinking the tea."

"True," said Pamela. "Whatever happened happened suddenly right after she drank that tea."

Rocky had reached their home and pulled into their garage. He slammed on the brakes with a start.

"Hey!" she shrieked. "Careful! You'll give me whiplash."

"Sorry," he replied, leaning back and turning to face her. "The tea."

"The tea? You mean, you think there was something wrong with the tea?" she asked. He stared at her.

"You're the detective," he noted. "Didn't it seem strange that she seemed completely fine until she drank from that tea cup and then she suddenly fell on the floor and died?"

"Yes," she said. "I told you I thought it was strange, but it's quite a leap to go from a person dying suddenly to—what? Are you suggesting that she was poisoned?"

"Maybe someone was jealous of her getting that part," he suggested.

"Oh, sure," she said with a scowl. "A role in an old drawing room comedy in a community theater production in a small southern town. People are just falling all over each other to get a part like that."

"You laugh," he said, "but you never know what motivates some people."

"I suppose," she said. A silence ensued as the two gathered their belongings and headed into their home. They ceased conversing as they hung up their jackets and changed clothes. Their small white poodle, Candide, was nowhere in sight; it was probably too late even for him to provide his typical greeting.

"Shall I make us some specialty beverages?" he asked as they got undressed.

"That depends," she replied. "Alcoholic?"

"Do you require alcohol, my dear?" he asked with a charming leer.

"No, actually, something more comforting seems appropriate," she said, as she thought back on the evening's events. "Something warm. I've suddenly got a chill."

"Coming right up," he replied and headed into their kitchen where she could hear him puttering around. The kitchen was Rocky's domain and he could spend hours there as he concocted wonderful new dishes for her to try. She was happy to be his food guinea pig, particularly because the entire idea of cooking was totally boring to her. Theirs was a topsy turvy arrangement if ever there was one. Of course, even though Rocky was the family cook, she couldn't say that she was the family handyman (or handyperson). True, she did "bring home the bacon" in that she made more money than Rocky, but that was simply not an issue with them. They had devised their agreeable division of chores primarily because Rocky loved all kitchen activities and she didn't—and there didn't seem any reason to change things around.

She pulled on her large fuzzy robe and matching slippers and plopped herself on their comfy bed. She arranged the throw pillows so she could lean back. Rocky soon entered with two tall mugs from which rose little puffs of steam.

"Shangri-La shakes," he announced, handing her one of the drinks.

"Ooo!" she said in delight. "This looks yummy."

"It's warm," he said. "And tropical, all at the same time."

"Sounds perfect," she said. "Oh no!"

"What?" he asked.

"Sounds!" she replied.

"Yes?"

"I just remembered that I have that audio recording still running in my purse. I forgot all about it when that poor woman...collapsed." She set down the mug, leaped from the bed, and ran over to a chair where she'd set her purse. She reached into the side pocket and drew out the small audio recorder. Turning it over, she pushed a black button on the front. "There! I turned it off. It recorded the whole thing, I guess. Even when the actress...collapsed. And the doctor. And when the director sent the audience home. Everything."

"I guess you'd better hang onto it," he said.

"Why?" she asked. "It's gruesome to think that I have this recording of the death of this poor woman."

"But if it does turn out to be a poisoning, surely the police will want to listen to it," he said.

"Why?" she asked. "There's no sound involved in a poisoning. Other than the sound the victim makes, I mean. The choking sounds which everyone heard. If it really was a poisoning.  And we don't know that, Rocky. It could be a natural death."

"It could be," he agreed, "but I can't help thinking that it occurred while Pamela Barnes—local acoustics expert and part-time detective—was there, and while she was actually recording the event.  Surely that can't be a coincidence?"

"You mean it was fate that I happened to record that production?" she asked.

"My dear," he said, coming over to where she was standing.  "I may not like the fact that you get involved in police investigations, but I'll have to admit that you have a knack for getting to the truth in these situations.  I just hope that this will not turn out to be one of those situations.  If it is, you'd best be prepared."

"So you think this little audio recording could turn out to be a vital clue in a murder investigation?"

"I wouldn't throw it away if I were you," he said firmly and clicked his mug to hers.

## CHAPTER 3

The next morning in her cheery office on the second floor of Blake Hall on the Grace University campus, Pamela was deep in thought. As usual, she was seated on her paisley love seat with her feet up. She had strategically placed her low heels on the floor beside her just in case a student showed up. Then she could quickly slip them on and appear immediately professional. But as apparently no such student was on the horizon, she was using her free office hour time to contemplate the events of the previous evening.

It was late morning and the halls outside her office seemed deserted. At least, she couldn't hear any of the normal between class chatter that usually filled them during the day. As she sipped the boysenberry tea from her thermos that Rocky had packed in her lunch, she detected the sound of high heels clicking down the echoing corridor. *Certainly not a student*, she mused. *They typically don't wear high heels, at least not to class.*

Her assessment of the sound was accurate and her friend and colleague Joan Bentley suddenly and dramatically appeared in the doorway. *Yes,* thought Pamela, *I understand why Joan would want to be in a theatrical production. She certainly has a dramatic flair about her.*

"Can you believe it, Pamela?" pronounced Joan, her arms outstretched as if she were a queen summoning her courtiers with just a flick of her pinkies.  "The entire production ruined!"

Pamela sat up on her couch but made no attempt to put on her shoes.

"Joan, a woman is dead."

"Yes," replied Joan still frozen mid-pose in the doorway. "I know, I know!  But right at the beginning of the show!  We didn't even get one night in.  Not even any time for a review or some publicity.  It's so terribly unfair."  Joan dropped her arms and her shoulders fell too.  She looked like a balloon that had suddenly been deflated.  She dragged herself over to the straight back chair beside the doorway and sank into it.

"It seems far more unfair to the poor woman who died," noted Pamela diplomatically.  Joan was a good and loyal friend but she was unabashedly vain, which was probably a necessity for any successful academic––and no doubt for any actress too.

"Yes, of course," continued Joan.  "Very sad, but so untimely."  She sighed and shook her head.

"Untimely?"

"I mean, she could have waited until the second night to flop dead in front of me," said Joan.

"Joan, that sounds heartless.  Don't you have any consideration for this person?  I mean, you were in a play with her; you surely got to know her.  You played her mother in the show, for heaven's sake!"  Pamela couldn't believe that Joan was saying what she was saying.

"I know, I know," said her friend, shaking her head of neat silver curls.  "It's simply horrible.  I'm just devastated, of course, for Belinda...she's the young woman who died.  A charming young girl.  Of course, I really didn't know her all that well. I spent more time conversing with other cast mates..."

"You mean, the men?" asked Pamela lifting an eyebrow.

"You know me, Pamela," said Joan with a shrug. "But Belinda was sweet...and a very good actress. Well, you saw that...at least for a brief period."

"Yes," replied Pamela, "she is...was...very good. Do you...know what happened? Was she ill?"

"No," said Joan, now crossing one neatly stockinged leg over the other. She wore patent leather pumps a bit higher than Pamela's lower heeled and more comfortable variety. Joan always dressed professionally but stylishly, and today she sported a green twill skirt with a plum-colored chiffon blouse topped off by a soft bow at the neck. Although her appearance was one of great propriety, Pamela knew that her friend had a wild side, but was always circumspect about her behavior and would never do anything to jeopardize her prestigious position as Graduate Coordinator in Grace's Psychology Department.

"So what do you...or *they* think happened?" Pamela asked.

"I don't know," replied Joan, rising and pacing around Pamela's desk on the other side of her office near her window. Joan leaned against the window frame and peered down at the campus below. "You were there. You saw everything I did. The doctor in the audience tried to revive her, but he couldn't."

"That's when we left," said Pamela. "I mean, that's when that man..."

"Ronald," said Joan, now sitting on the edge of the desk. "He's our director. He's wonderful!"

"Anyway," continued Pamela, "when he told everyone to leave, we left, obviously. Did anything happen after that?"

"Not really," Joan said, fingering some pencils in a container on the desk. "The police arrived shortly after that. I guess because it was a sudden death."

"Yes, that makes sense," said Pamela. "They usually do that. What did they say?"

"Nothing to us actors," said Joan. "They made us wait forever! The coroner came and took Belinda's body away."

"What about those two people who were in the audience?" asked Pamela, bending forward. "You know; the man and the woman who were sitting across from Rocky and me? They both ran onto the stage when the woman...Belinda...collapsed. I assume they knew her?"

"It was her mother and husband," replied Joan. "I didn't know them personally. Belinda was a newlywed."

"Oh no!" exclaimed Pamela. "How horrible for the husband!"

"Yes," said Joan, now roaming back across the office and sitting down again on the chair. "I believe he's a local car dealer. You know, Purvis Autos."

"Oh, yes!" said Pamela, "Out on the highway."

"I don't pay much attention to such things," said Joan, looking around distracted.

"It's quite large," said Pamela. "You've driven by there, surely. He's that Purvis?"

"The son of the owner, I think," said Joan. "I believe I overheard one of the cast members discussing him and Belinda once. I really didn't pay that much attention. We did our scenes together. We practiced but the only thing we really discussed together was the show—and our characters.  She was really excited about being in the play.  I gather she'd never acted before."

"Just like you," said Pamela, with a knowing glance at her friend.

"I may not have ever acted before, Pamela," noted Joan, rising again and continuing her walk around the small office, "but I have a lengthy career as a professor, and you and I both know that teaching is a lot like acting.  Or at least, one needs to be a good actor to be a good teacher."

"I agree with you there," said Pamela with a laugh. Joan was right that the best teachers were those who realized that teaching was more than simply imparting information.  They realized that to truly educate and inspire students they needed to engage them and motivate them—something that probably required some acting skill.  If Pamela's students were to be believed, Joan was one of the best instructors in the department—her classes were lively, informative, and fun.

"So, this acting thing came naturally to you?" she asked.

"Like falling off the academic log," replied Joan with a wink.  "And of course, I have a photographic memory, so learning lines was a breeze.  I don't see why it's so difficult for so many. I had to help many of the cast members learn their lines. Poor dears!"  She looked out the window wistfully.

"My guess here—the male cast members?" asked Pamela.

"Hmm," said Joan. "I guess. They do seem to have more trouble with words than we do, don't they?" She gave Pamela a devilish smile and returned to her chair.

"So," said Pamela, sitting up and pressing her hands together. "Do they plan to restage? Or cancel? Or what?"

"Bite your tongue on that cancel, my dear," snapped Joan. "We certainly didn't go through all that work for nothing. I'm sure we'll find a new Gwendolyn and restage. I mean, we have to do it for Reardon, for the Community Theater, for the Coffee Factory. We have so many people counting on us."

"I'm glad to hear that," replied Pamela. "How long do you think this will all take?"

"Of course, there will have to be a discreet period of mourning—for Belinda," said Joan, "but we can't wait too long or the rest of us will forget our lines and our blocking."

"Blocking?" asked Pamela.

"Our stage movement," replied Joan, severely. "I know! Maybe you could play Belinda!"

"Bite your tongue," said Pamela quickly. "I have absolutely no interest in acting!"

"Too busy detecting, hmm?" asked Joan.

"I'd much rather be in the audience cheering you on!" she argued. "And next time, I can be there with Arliss, hopefully. Not Rocky. He's a stick in the mud. You'd think that someone who teaches English would love to go see live theater."

"That's just men, my dear," said Joan, fluffing her chiffon tie. "Theater is not considered manly. You have to work with them to change these antiquated ideas."

"Something I'm sure you're very good at," said Pamela laughing.

"I try," replied Joan with a lilt. "But truly, Pamela, let's hope that by the time the show is ready to go again, Arliss will be able to accompany you instead of your recalcitrant husband. I know she was anxious to see my performance and now she'll actually get to go to opening night—sort of."

"A good way to look at it," said Pamela with a nod.

The office phone rang and Pamela rose and walked to her desk and answered it.

"Hello?" she said into the receiver. "Hi, Arliss."

"Tell her I was wonderful in the play," whispered Joan.

"Yes," said Pamela back into the phone. "Joan's here now. She says to tell you she was wonderful." She gave Joan a cheesy smile. Then she listened as Arliss asked a question. "Yes, I recorded it, but unfortunately, I didn't get the entire performance."

She nodded and smiled at Joan as the two women waited for Arliss's reply.

"Listen, Arliss," said Pamela into the receiver when Arliss had finished talking. "The reason I didn't get the entire performance is because the show never concluded. Right in the middle of the first act, one of the actresses collapsed on stage—and died!"

Joan was standing a few feet from the telephone, but even she could hear Arliss's voice scream, "Oh no! How's Joan?"

"Fine," said Pamela quickly into the phone. "Joan is fine. But the woman who died was the woman who played her daughter. She collapsed during a scene with Joan. They were seated at a table drinking tea and all of a sudden this young woman clutched her throat and then fell to the floor in a heap. Everyone in the audience was stunned. For a second, no one was sure if it was part of the show."

"What!" yelled Joan, motioning wildly to Pamela. "Why would we have someone die during 'The Importance of Being Earnest'?"

Pamela was suddenly feeling a bit dizzy trying to follow Arliss's questions on the telephone and Joan's frantic, whispered comments from the other side of her desk.

"Yes, yes," she said into the phone. "I tell you Joan is fine. No, I don't know why the woman died. No one does, but Joan says the police were called in. There will probably be an autopsy. Hopefully we'll know something eventually."

"Doesn't she want to know about the play?" whispered Joan hoarsely, waving her hands at Pamela.

"Oh, yes, the play!" said Pamela into the receiver. "Joan says to tell you that they intend to reschedule the play as soon as they can find someone to take the part of Gwendolyn. That's the role of the woman who died. Do you want to play her?"

"What!" shouted Joan.

"Sorry," said Pamela to the phone and Joan. "I guess they're desperate to find a replacement since Joan just asked *me*." She laughed and apparently Arliss laughed too on the other end. Joan stood with her hands on her hips. "Arliss says to tell you that if you think she'd ever be in a play, you're a monkey's uncle! And she knows her monkeys!"

## CHAPTER 4

Several days later, Pamela and Rocky were in their bedroom watching the late night local news. Their tiny poodle Candide was snuggled between the two, getting head rubs from his two favorite humans.

"The coroner's office reports that Belinda Purvis, the young woman who died suddenly during the opening night of Reardon Community Theater's production of 'The Importance of Being Earnest,' did not die of natural causes. Toxicology reports are pending," said the young reporter standing in front of the Coffee Factory, with a poster for the show visible directly behind her. "Police suspect foul play at this time."

"Oh, no!" cried Pamela. "She *was* poisoned. Just as we suspected, Rocky." She turned to her husband who put his finger to his lips as he continued to watch the on-screen report.

"I'm talking with Ron Whitcomb, the show's director," said the young woman as the camera focused on the face of the tall man Pamela had seen the previous evening come onto the stage. "Mr. Whitcomb, do you have any idea who could have done this to Miss Purvis? Did she have any enemies?"

"Absolutely not," said Whitcomb, his eyes bloodshot and his face drained of vitality. "Belinda was a sweet, charming girl—delightful like her character in the play. I can't imagine her having any enemies.  She was recently married to Matt Purvis, who's just heartbroken. She was a newlywed, for God's sake.  I just can't understand it at all."  He shook his head and squinted at the ground.

"Do the police have any idea who might have done this?" continued the aggressive reporter.  "Not that they've told me," said Whitcomb.  "The whole cast is in shock.  We all loved Belinda."

"This was your opening night, wasn't it?" prompted the reporter as Whitcomb continued to stare at the ground.

"It was," he replied.  "A really big night not just for the Reardon Community Theater, but for the entire town as well.  With the theater relocated here on the upper floor of the Coffee Factory, we hoped to see a revival of both the theater and the downtown area.  A plus for both groups—and for residents and tourists alike."   Pamela thought that this sounded like the theater director's sales pitch and was probably a speech he was accustomed to giving.  She'd heard Joan present a similar argument many times.

"So," said the reporter, "this puts a crimp in your plans, doesn't it?  I mean, what are you going to do now?"

"My plans," said Whitcomb with annoyance, "you mean *our* plans...are on hold for now.  Our first priority is to aid the police in finding out who did this to Belinda and assist her family in any way we can.  Only secondarily are we concerned with the production.  Yes, eventually we want to restage—but that's a goal for the future.  Right now we are devoted to Belinda and her family."

*Yay!* thought Pamela, *this man is certainly more diplomatic a spokesperson for the Reardon Community*

*Theater than Joan. Of course, Joan probably would say something like this if she were speaking on camera.*

"That's the guy from the show," noted Rocky. "The one who called the doctor."

"Yes, the director," said Pamela. "Joan told me about him."

"He seems on top of things," added Rocky as Candide licked his hand and begged for more head scratching. Rocky obliged. "Hey, Buddy, be patient." Turning to Pamela, he asked, "What else did she say?"

"Not much," noted Pamela. "She said the police came and held the actors for a while but then eventually released them. Joan seems mostly concerned about when they can restage the production."

"She would," Rocky replied.

"What does that mean?" she snorted, crossing her arms. Candide jumped from his mistress's sudden movement.

"Nothing," he said, placing a calming hand on her arm. "You know, you'd think Joan would be more concerned about who poisoned the woman rather than when the show would be restaged. I mean, she was sitting next to her when this all happened. The woman died from poison that she drank from a cup. She poured it from a teapot on that table and Joan drank from a cup that she poured from that same teapot. Joan could have been poisoned too."

"Oh, my God, Rocky!" exclaimed Pamela. "You're right! I never even considered that. I have to call Joan!" Pamela rolled over to grab the telephone from her nightstand.

"What?" he cried. "No! Don't do that! You'll just upset her, Pamela. Obviously, she didn't drink any poison so any speculation after the fact is moot.  The police will certainly test the contents of both the cup and the teapot."

"I can't believe this didn't occur to her—or to me," said Pamela, scooting back over to sit beside her husband.

"Maybe it did occur to her and she's just too scared to mention it," he suggested.

"Joan is never too scared to do anything," said Pamela, shaking her head.  "And besides, the whole idea of this being a poisoning was all speculation until now.  Now that it's official and they've broadcast the autopsy report, we know for sure that's how Belinda died.  Now everyone will start to wonder how..."

"And who," he added.

"Yes, who," she agreed.  "Belinda was apparently sweet, and didn't seem to have any enemies.  Who would want to kill her?"

"Maybe no one wanted to kill her," he said.

"What do you mean?"

"I mean maybe someone just wanted to kill someone and Belinda just happened to be the one," he said.

"You mean like a serial killer?" she asked.  She pushed Candide off of her lap where he'd fallen asleep and turned towards her husband in an attempt to follow his train of thinking.

"Maybe someone was just angry and put poison in that teacup and didn't care who drank it," he argued.

"But that doesn't make sense, Rocky," she replied. "If that's the case, that person would be someone connected to the production and that person would surely know that the only people who would drink from that teapot would be Belinda and Joan."

"Maybe Belinda wasn't the intended victim," he said suddenly. "Maybe it was Joan."

"Oh, no!" she screamed. "Now I really must call Joan! What if that is the case? She could be in danger!" She clambered back to grab the phone.

"No!" he said. "Stop! That doesn't make sense either. If Joan was the intended target, why would the killer bother putting the poison in the pot? Then he'd be killing two people..."

"If he's a crazed killer, he wouldn't care how many people he killed," she argued.

"I think that's unlikely," he said. "My guess is that the killer succeeded in finding his target."

"And if you're wrong?" she queried.

"Then Joan is the probably the next victim," he said, then quickly added, "but I really think that's unlikely."

Pamela leaned back against the bed's headboard and closed her eyes. This was a frightening dilemma. Should she warn Joan about her concerns?

"And of course there's the other important fact," he said calmly.

"What?" she sighed.

"Most poisonings are done by women," he pronounced.

"That's just an old stereotype," she huffed. "Men are just as capable of poisoning someone as women."

"Capable, yes," he noted, "but less likely. Men, and here I include myself in this unfortunate group, tend to be more hotheaded and when we're angry we act violently without much thought."

Pamela laughed. Rocky was not always so self-deprecating.

"There's not a violent bone in your body," she said smiling at him, and then added, "although you do get angry a lot over many totally innocuous things."

"What?" he howled. "Innocuous? What about the time you let the water run so long in the bathtub that it ran over the edge and flooded the bathroom? We had to call out a plumber! It cost a fortune! Do you call that innocuous?"

"Maybe not," she squeaked, and ducked dramatically as if she expected a blow, "but you get furious if I don't recognize the name of some casserole you made years ago..."

"Not years ago, two weeks ago," he snorted. "And it was a delicious one that you raved over! You'd think you could at least remember what they're called when I go to all the trouble to make them for you!"

"Oh my!" she whispered, inhaling in spurts. "Rocky!" She looked at him sadly and he exhaled suddenly, totally deflated.

"See what I mean?" he whispered. "Men are inherently violent. We just explode when we're upset. We don't take the time and effort to plot revenge. Poisoning takes time and effort. Oh, I'm not saying a man can't be a poisoner, but I just think women are genetically more inclined to be poisoners rather than violent killers—if, of course, they're going to kill anyone at all."

"Maybe," she replied. "But I certainly know that I couldn't poison anyone—or kill them violently either, of course."

"Definitely you couldn't poison anyone," he said. She smiled benignly. Then he added, "Because it would involve mixing ingredients together and that's way too much like cooking—something I know you hate."

"True," she agreed. "And since you're such a good cook, I guess that makes you far more likely to be the poisoner in our family—even if you are male."

"All male. And don't you forget it," he said with a smile, biting her ear. As the nibbling got more amorous, Candide began to complain with little annoyed barks. Any romantic activity between his owners was invariably the precursor to his being evicted from their comfortable bed, and banished to the floor.

Pamela sat up suddenly.

"Rocky!" she exclaimed. "I'm sorry. I just can't stop thinking about Joan and how close she came to being a victim of that poisoner. I mean, if there was poison in the teapot and Joan poured it in her cup and drank from it, she'd be dead now. If there was poison only in a cup, how would the poisoner know which cup which woman would drink from?"

"Surely the cups were placed on the side of the table where each actress sat," he said.

"I don't know," she said, squeezing her forehead tightly as if to call up a memory that remained buried deeply in her brain. "I think the teapot and both cups were on a tray on the table. If I remember correctly, Joan poured the tea from the pot into each cup and then the women drank from them. Who knows which cup she would give to which person? Surely the poisoner must have put the poison in the pot, and not just one cup, otherwise he would run the risk of the wrong woman drinking it?"

"Are you sure that's what happened?" he asked.

"No," she whimpered. "I really wasn't paying any attention to who was pouring or drinking the tea. I was just enjoying the performance."

"You can ask Joan when you see her," he suggested quickly, obviously anxious to get back to ear nibbling.

"Okay," she agreed. "The last thing I need is to provoke you to violence."

He smiled rather wickedly.

**CHAPTER 5**

Pamela had barely entered the foyer of the main office of the Psychology Department the next morning when she bumped into Bob Goodman, a tall, gawky man made even more so by his inordinately skinny frame.  He rebalanced the stack of books he was carrying in one arm and tipped his glasses back up his long nose.

"Pamela," he greeted her.  "Arliss tells me you had quite an exciting evening the other night!"

"Indeed," responded Pamela.  "Arliss missed all the excitement staying home with your baby."

"Can't say I'd care to witness a poisoning death," he said bending closer to her in confidence as they both leaned down at the wall of cubbyholes which served as faculty mailboxes.

"No," she replied, "it was not what Rocky and I were expecting when we went there hoping to enjoy Joan's acting debut."  She pulled out several letters and a few flyers from her box.

"Excitement just seems to follow you, doesn't it, Pamela?" asked Bob, peering at her over the tops of his glasses.  She looked up at him.  Was Arliss's husband worried about his wife's friends and their activities?  Maybe now that the couple had a child he would be extra circumspect in his concern for Arliss.

Pamela's reverie was interrupted by the departmental secretary, Jane Marie, who popped her head into the main office from her small alcove that stood between it and the office of their Department Head, Mitchell Marks. Jane Marie smiled broadly at the two faculty members, her head of curly brown locks bobbing up and down as she spoke.

"Dr. Goodman, Dr. Barnes!" she greeted them. "Good morning! Dr. Barnes, are you on the trail of the person who poisoned that poor woman in that show?"

"Oh, Jane Marie!" exclaimed Pamela, following the secretary into her small office. She plopped down on a chair opposite the desk that was crammed in front of a large window overlooking a grassy walkway where passing students could be seen and heard. "Let's not go there!" Jane Marie was always anxious to follow Pamela's detecting adventures and had even aided her in the past with tracking down important clues.

"She was there!" noted Bob as he followed the two women into Jane Marie's office. He remained standing in the doorway. "Thank heavens Arliss was home with Noah and didn't have to witness such a horrible event." He leaned against the doorframe as he examined his mail.

"You both realize that the person who witnessed the horrible event close up was Joan," Pamela said to them. "She actually knew the woman who died. She played her mother in the production."

"I can't imagine how terrible that must have been for both you—and Dr. Bentley!" exclaimed Jane Marie, now having moved her rolling office chair behind her desk. Pamela often thought that not many individuals would be able to make such a small desk in such a small office appear as cozy and individualized as Jane Marie had. The decorations changed from season to season and Jane Marie's entire life and complete family held a position on at least a portion of the available wall space.  As it was fall, Jane Marie had a leaf motif going on, dominated by colors of orange and rust.

"Have you spoken to Joan?" asked Bob.

"Yes, yesterday," she said.  "Of course, when I talked to her neither of us knew for certain that the girl had actually been poisoned.  I only found that out last night when I heard the autopsy report on television, but she and I both thought that it was very suspicious."

"How so?" asked Bob.  "Did the woman say something?"

"No," said Pamela, "she just made noises.  But she certainly seemed just fine right up until she collapsed on stage.  And Joan said there had been no mention whatsoever of her having any sort of medical condition."

"Do the police have any clues?" asked Jane Marie, clutching a felt turkey that she had displayed prominently on her desk.  Pamela assumed it had been made by one of her children.

"You would know as much as I do," said Pamela. "They didn't say anything on the news last night.  Just that the autopsy indicated that she had been poisoned."

At that last word, the closed door on the other side of Jane Marie's little alcove opened suddenly and a large, elegant man with wavy blond hair and striking blue eyes appeared in the entrance.

"Poisoned?" he stated as he glanced around at each person in Jane Marie's small office.  "I might have known I'd find you in here, Pamela, if the discussion is murder."

"Dr. Marks," said Jane Marie, putting down the little turkey, and turning to her boss. "Surely you heard that Dr. Barnes was at that play the other night where that woman died? You know, the one that Dr. Bentley was in?"

"Oh, yes," noted Marks, moving over to the corner of the secretary's desk and leaning against it. His smart grey herringbone suit set him off as dressed much more elegantly than the members of his department. "That's Joan for you, I guess. She's certainly involved in a lot of local activities."

"She's on the board of directors of the theater," added Pamela.

"I'll bet she's fabulous in the play," gushed Jane Marie.

"Oh, she is!" agreed Pamela. "It's really too bad that all this happened. It was such a delightful show; I just know it would have been very successful...if not for the...you know." She shrugged. It seemed in bad form, somehow, to be lauding Joan's performance in light of the horrific events of opening night.

The four people in the room all looked down. Eventually the silence was broken by Marks.

"So, Pamela," he said, almost brightly. "I assume you'll be solving this murder—or at least aiding the police in their efforts."

"No," she replied, ever so slightly annoyed. "Not this time, Mitchell. There's no sound aspect to this crime. It's a poisoning, after all. Oh, the victim did make choking sounds when she collapsed, but that's hardly a clue to the murderer."

"She didn't try to say someone's name?" asked Bob. "I mean, maybe she realized as she was dying who did it? Do you think?"

"I don't," said Pamela. "It all happened so fast, I don't think she had any time to think about anything."

"But you were there, Pamela," said Mitchell, pointing at her. "And when you're around a murder scene, I'm convinced your investigative juices start to flow." He crossed his arms and nodded.

"Yes, Dr. Barnes," agreed Jane Marie. "I bet you saw something or—better yet—heard something that happened during the show or before the show that will give you a clue to solving this mystery."

"I don't think so," she said with a shrug. She was not going to be roped into working on another murder investigation. She had much too much to do with her regular work—her students, her classes, her committee assignments, and, most of all, her research.

"Oh, give it up, Pamela," said Bob, shaking his head. "You're the department's Sherlock Holmes and everyone here expects you to solve this case."

"Expectations that, I'm sorry to say, will not be met," she said pointedly, standing up and gathering her belongings.

"So, you're saying you didn't see or hear anything at the production that might be a clue to the killer?" asked Mitchell. His blue eyes stared at her directly as if willing her to respond in a particular way.

"Just what would I have seen or heard?" she asked with frustration, looking around the small room.

"If the woman was poisoned, Dr. Barnes," said Jane Marie, leaning forward, "the killer had to get the poison to her."

"It was probably in the tea cup she was drinking from during the scene," said Pamela to the secretary. "She seemed fine before she drank from the cup and when she did drink from it, she became immediately ill."

"And the police found poison in the cup?" asked Bob.

"The reporter only said that she was poisoned, not where the poison was found or anything else," said Pamela. "And even if they did, whoever did it probably did it backstage where I wouldn't have seen anything."

"Because you were in the audience," said Jane Marie.

"Did you get a good look at this woman when she collapsed?" asked Marks.

"Actually, yes," said Pamela. "It was theater in the round, you know. She was seated quite close to us. She and Joan were performing a little scene at a table that was set almost in front of our seats, so when she fell, she couldn't have been more than a few feet away from me."

"Truly a front row seat," said Bob Goodman thoughtfully. "A front row seat to murder."

"Oh my!" exclaimed Jane Marie. "What if Dr. Bentley had sipped the poison tea? Didn't you say they were both drinking tea in the scene?"

"Yes," said Pamela. "This part I don't remember exactly. I remember Joan pouring tea for the two of them. I remember Joan drinking from her cup and the other woman drinking from her cup. I think. Maybe there was no pouring and they both just drank. I'll be certain to ask Joan when I see her. She can tell me. Then I can get her to tell me more about Belinda too."

"Belinda?" asked Jane Marie.

"Yes, Belinda Purvis," said Pamela, "the young actress who died. I understand from Joan that she was a newlywed.  She was married to Tom Purvis, of Purvis Autos."

"I know her!" shouted Jane Marie.  "She used to be Belinda Whatley.  She was a student here at Grace.  I even believe she took some courses here.  Such a nice young woman."

"You know," added Mitchell, "I believe I remember having a Belinda Whatley in one of my Intro classes several years ago.  That was probably her.  How sad.  Come to think of it now, I'm sure I remember her.  A sweet girl, hardworking, conscientious.  Who in the world would want to kill such a nice young woman?"

"Who indeed?" asked Pamela.  Her heart trembled.  It was bad enough having witnessed this young woman's death, but discovering that she had been a Grace alum and had taken courses in her department, Pamela felt more and more as if she had just lost a relative.  She wondered why Joan hadn't mentioned these facts about Belinda.  *Of course, maybe Joan didn't know that Belinda had taken courses in the Psychology Department, although you'd think that the young woman would surely have mentioned that fact to Joan when they'd become acquainted.  Oh, well, this is all speculation, and none of it will help discover Belinda's killer.*

*Discover Belinda's killer?*  She had resolved not to think like this; she had promised her husband that her detecting days were over.  And here she was contemplating possible clues that might lead her to discovering another murderer.

She bid farewell to Jane Marie and Mitchell and walked with Bob out the main office door.

"I hope Noah is feeling better," she said to him.

"Much," he replied. "Poor Arliss was going stir-crazy for a while there. You'll probably see her today. She's desperate for adult companionship."

"I can hardly wait," she replied. And it was true, she could hardly wait. Arliss was a dear friend and she missed her company. She had a lot to tell her.

## CHAPTER 6

Pamela hadn't seen either of her two friends—Joan or Arliss—during the morning, which wasn't unusual as they both had classes.  As she walked leisurely back to her office from her last morning class, she was primarily contemplating lunch—specifically what her husband had packed for her lunch today.  Each day was a delightful mystery.  He typically made some unusual sandwich with some sort of side salad in a plastic container.  Sometimes he included a dessert—but not often.  And, of course, her thermos always contained some new exotic brand of tea.  Today's was orange honey and she'd already downed most of it as she lectured during her two morning classes.

She unlocked her door and entered her homey domain.  Quickly she dropped her clipboard and lecture notes on her desk, grabbed her lunch sack, and plopped herself down on her sofa, ready to open the sack and savor the contents.  Today, Rocky had prepared a whole wheat sandwich with a strange filling.  She couldn't quite put her finger on the flavors in the light green spread.  *Hmm*, she wondered, *a hint of lime and maybe, avocado.  But there's something else in here too.*  She'd have to ask Rocky when she got home because this little culinary mystery was almost superseding the big mystery that had been dominating her thoughts.  The poisoning death of Belinda Purvis. It was probably a good thing that she was able to put her mind on other topics.  After all, it was sad, but it wasn't her problem and she did have a job and students who needed her attention.

As she contemplated the nature of the sandwich filling, the sound of two female voices she recognized drifted towards her from down the hallway.  As it was lunch time, most students were out of class and no doubt, out of the building.  The two voices were chatting with animation and getting louder when suddenly Joan Bentley and a younger woman appeared in Pamela's doorway.  Today Joan was resplendent in a stylish mauve suit with a green printed blouse.  The young woman beside her was a distinct contrast, wearing nondescript, loose trousers that hung over the tops of her dilapidated sneakers.  The only nod she seemed to give to professional attire was the plain white, button-down blouse and a bland, brown jacket. Her blouse was not tucked in and hung around her hips.  The woman's hair was a mass of black frizzy curls that she appeared to be attempting to rein in— unsuccessfully—with a black hair band.

"Arliss!  Joan!" announced Pamela to her friends as she sat up on her couch.  She motioned them to come inside.   Arliss  stormed  in,  rounded  the  desk,  and plopped down in Pamela's desk chair, uninvited and as if she had sat there on many occasions. Joan followed her at a more dignified pace and sat on her apparently favorite straight back chair by the door, hands demurely on her lap.  "How's Noah?" Pamela asked Arliss, who had now placed her feet on Pamela's desk.

"I'm exhausted!" she announced to the two women with a sigh.  "Babies are tiring enough, but when they're sick, it's twice as bad!"

"You knew what you were getting yourself in for," noted Joan primly with a slight shaking of her finger.

"No, I didn't, Joan!" declared Arliss. "I assumed that babies wouldn't be any harder to care for than animals. I can take care of a laboratory full of critters with much less effort than one little boy!"

"You love it, Arliss," said Pamela. She cringed as Arliss's feet smashed a stack of her student papers in the middle of her desk. "Noah is adorable!"

"Not when he's dripping snot," replied Arliss with a shake of her head. The massive mop of black frizz shook when she spoke.

"Ah, motherhood!" said Joan serenely. "It brings back so many fond memories."

"Joan," Arliss said, glaring at her friend across the room, "I can't imagine you putting up with sick babies; you probably hired a nanny to take them out in a pram when they got so much as a sniffle."

"Maybe I did," she said. "It's so long ago, I can hardly remember." She smiled benignly at Arliss. "I'm sure Pamela can recall sick days; after all, she's a bit younger than me."

"A bit," said Pamela, slightly amused at the apparent battle over the nature of mothering a sick child that was raging between her two friends. "Of course, I only have the one. And she's an adult now."

"You two!" scowled Arliss. "You know exactly what I'm going through. You're just trying to pretend that it's all natural when it's really horrible!"

"Really, Arliss," said Joan, now all business and bending forward in lecture mode. "You can't expect a human baby to behave the same way as a baby...monkey! Or a baby guinea pig!"

"I don't!" howled Arliss, now shoving herself backwards on Pamela's rolling desk chair. "Of course I love Noah! But, I never figured he'd need so much constant attention. I mean, with lab animals, you feed them and clean their cages and that's about it."

"I certainly hope you do more for Noah than just feed him," said Pamela.

"And clean his cage!" added Joan, with a devilish glint.

"You know what I mean, Joan!" whined Arliss, rolling back to the desk and plopping her fluffy head in her hands on Pamela's desk blotter.

"Oh, Arliss," said Pamela sweetly. "We're just teasing you. You have our sympathy, truly you do. Motherhood is never easy. Particularly because mothers end up doing so much more than fathers!"

"It's true!" yelled Arliss, lifting her head. "Bob just complains about Noah's condition, but when I think about it, he doesn't really do anything to help me."

"Welcome to the world," said Joan. "If men had to take care of sick babies, daycare workers would make a lot more money."

"And I missed Joan's performance!" added Arliss. "I really wanted to see it!"

"Joan was fabulous!" said Pamela, smiling sideways at Joan, who blushed noticeably and tittered.

"Of course, you'll get your chance to see me, my dear," said Joan, "because it appears we will be redoing our opening night."

"I can't believe someone actually died right during the performance," said Arliss, now totally engrossed in Joan's story, her baby's illness apparently forgotten.

"Not just died," said Pamela, "poisoned!"

"They're sure?" asked Arliss.

"Yes," said Pamela, cringing as Arliss slung her feet back on the desk. "They announced the autopsy report on television last night. Didn't you hear it?"

"When do I have time to watch TV?" asked Arliss, visibly feeling sorry for herself as she jutted out her lower lip in defiance of her motherly obligations.

"Have the police contacted you again, Joan?" asked Pamela.

"No," replied Joan. "They only spoke to the cast and crew as a group the night of the show and then let us go. Of course, then, no one knew that Belinda had been poisoned. Only that she had died suddenly. Now that they know she was poisoned, I assume they'll probably be around to ask us more questions. After all, it's now a murder investigation." She rubbed her hands together and nibbled her lower lip.

"Have you thought any more about why anyone would want to hurt that young woman?" Pamela asked Joan.

"I haven't," replied Joan. "I haven't the foggiest. As I said to you the other day, Pamela, I really never even talked much with her except to run lines. She seemed like a nice young woman. Most of what she said seemed to revolve around her husband. She was a newlywed. Always, 'Matt' this or 'Matt' that! You know how some women are! So one-track minded."

Indeed, Pamela did know how some women were.

"Jane Marie said that she'd been a Grace student," said Pamela. "That she'd even taken courses in our department. Mitchell remembered having her in class."

"Really?" asked Joan.

"Yes," replied Pamela. "That would have been before she was married—you did say she was a newlywed, didn't you?  I believe Jane Marie said her maiden name was Whatley.  Belinda Whatley."

"What did Mitchell say about her?" asked Arliss.

"Not much except that she was a good student and a pleasant young woman," replied Pamela, "certainly nothing that would be grounds for murder."

"If she was even the intended target?" mused Pamela as she continued to sip her tea from her thermos, looking at Joan quizzically.

"What do you mean by that, Pamela?" asked Joan with a distinct frown.

"I was just curious, Joan," she said, "about how the poisoning occurred.  Haven't you thought about it?  I mean you were sitting there at that little table on stage with the victim.  She was poisoned, I'm assuming from a substance in the tea she drank.  Well, you drank from that same teapot.  Haven't you thought at all about why you weren't poisoned too?"

"Oh, that!" replied Joan flippantly.  "That couldn't have happened because there wasn't anything in the teapot."

"No tea?" asked Arliss.

"No," said Joan.  "I just faked pouring it.  We tried it at one rehearsal with liquid in the pot and me actually pouring it, but it was confusing and—truth be told—I'm terrible at pouring tea particularly when I'm trying to stay in character and recite my lines.  So finally, Ron, the director, just said leave the teapot empty and just put a little liquid in each cup so when we drank, there would actually be something in our cups. The crew always put a little iced tea in each of our cups before each rehearsal.  It worked fine and Belinda and I liked it that way.  Belinda actually liked her tea plain, but I liked mine with a little lemon in it.  That's how we told our cups apart on stage actually. Mine had the lemon slice on the saucer. It was actually really nice because if my throat got a little dry, I'd have a supply of cold, lemony liquid to sip at the ready."

"Now I see," said Pamela mysteriously, nodding slowly.

"Now you see what, Pam?" asked Arliss, tuning in to her friend's new mood.

"I see why Joan didn't feel threatened by Belinda's poisoning as there was no reason for her to be frightened of poison in Belinda's cup which was prepared totally separately from hers. Also, I see how the killer used this knowledge to hone in on his or her target. The killer must have known which cup on the table Belinda would use—the prop crew placed the cup without the lemon slice on the side of the table where Belinda sat. There wasn't any need to put poison in the tea pot. Actually, not only did this allow the killer to avoid killing anyone other than the intended victim, but it also allowed the killer the opportunity to put the full strength amount of poison in the victim's cup where she would drink a massive dose and not have it diluted by putting it in the pot and having the victim only drink a small portion from that pot."

"My goodness, Pamela," said Joan, "I see you're already in investigative mode."

"I wish I'd been there," sighed Arliss. "It must have been so exciting!"

"Oh," exclaimed Pamela suddenly, rising and going to her desk where her pocketbook rested. "Speaking of your not being there! I made that audio recording for you, Arliss. You can take it with you and listen to the opening of the show if you like, at least up until

Belinda collapses and they cancel the performance."
She opened her purse and started to rummage inside,
looking for the audio recorder.

"Never mind, my dear!" proclaimed Joan.  "There's
no reason for her to listen to just a portion of it.  You
just wait until we restage, Arliss.  Then, you can *see* —
not just hear—the entire production from start to
finish."

"Okay," agreed Arliss.  "You keep the recording,
Pam.  I'd really rather see it live, if you don't mind."

"I don't mind at all," replied Pamela, setting the
recorder she had just found on her desk and returning
to her comfy couch.

## CHAPTER 7

Several hours later, Pamela was seated at her desk attempting to grade a batch of student quizzes.  Her afternoon office hours had remained as quiet as the morning ones and, except for the earlier visit from Joan and Arliss, she had accomplished a lot today.  She leaned back in her desk chair and took a deep breath.  Glancing up, she noticed the pocket audio recorder that she had removed earlier from her purse.  Since Arliss would not be using this recording, mused Pamela, she might as well clear it.  She reached across her desk to pick up the small device.  As she turned it over in her hands and started to punch the 'rewind' button, she thought back to Rocky's earlier admonition that she should hang on to the recording in case the police might want to use it.

*Oh, that was silly!* was her first reaction to his warning.  There couldn't be any information on this audio recording that would assist the police.  She watched the small wheels spin furiously as the tape ran back to the start of the recording.

When the recorder had returned to the beginning, she hit the 'play' button and listened to the conversation she remembered having with Rocky right before the beginning of the performance.  *I doubt that there's any pertinent information in this segment,* she thought to herself.  She pushed the 'fast forward' button and the recorder spun ahead.  She pressed 'stop' and the device ended abruptly.  She hit 'play' again and this time she heard a segment of the performance that she remembered as occurring in the first scene.  Here she could hear the actors and actresses who had played the main characters.  Joan sounded larger than life, as she always did—on stage and off.

She ran the recording ahead again, this time in a shorter burst, not wanting to run past the moment where Belinda Purvis died.  When she hit 'play' this time, she discovered that she was apparently in the blackout right before the deadly scene.  She assumed this because there was no dialogue taking place and only soft background music playing.  She could hear a lot of noise, mostly whispered conversation from herself and Rocky and probably audience members seated next to them and behind them.  As they had been in the front row, those were the only locations possible for audience members to be around them. She could also at times hear some stage noises, such as glasses tinkling or furniture being moved.  It was actually quite remarkable that there wasn't more stage noise, she noted, and that the stage crew was able to move the props around as they did with so little noise in the dark.  It probably took quite a bit of rehearsal just to be able to do all of that so quickly and quietly. She grabbed a pen and paper and wrote down the number on the recorder that indicated where the blackout occurred on her audio recording.  Then she continued to listen, also adding on her paper the number that denoted where the blackout ended and where the stage lights came up (or at least where she believed the stage lights came up as she couldn't see them do so just by listening to her audio recording).

The second scene began and Pamela noted the audio recorder location number for this point too on her list. She continued to listen and when the dialogue between Joan and Belinda began—the one that Pamela realized would suddenly conclude when the young woman collapsed—she marked its beginning also. She listened now even more carefully, attempting to determine if she could note exactly when Belinda drank the fateful dose of poison. She replayed a few sections several times, being clued by a choking sound that she believed had been made by Belinda—at least that's what she remembered. She marked this moment too on her paper by noting its location on the recorder's timer.

The recorder continued to play as she clutched the little black device in her hands. Pamela relived the events of the night that she still recalled with horror. She could hear Belinda's body hit the stage floor. She could hear gasps from audience members. She could hear the authoritative, but stunned, voice of the director Ron Whitcomb as he called for a physician and then eventually requested the audience to quietly leave. Then, of course, she realized that the recording continued for a much longer time as it recorded her conversation with Rocky in their car and even later when they were at home. She marked down the point on the tape when she and Rocky actually left the theater because she believed that from that point on, no more pertinent information could be derived from it regarding the death of the young actress, Belinda Purvis—Belinda Whatley Purvis, has some of her colleagues might remember her.

Winding the recorder back to the location where the play began, she pressed 'play' and listened again, this time concentrating more carefully on not just the speeches of the actors and actresses, but on any ambient sounds that the recorder picked up. She knew, as an acoustics expert, that often the most valuable clues lay in the most unexpected places and the most unexpected sounds. Possibly there was a noise on this recording that would clue her to the person who had killed Belinda. Obviously it was someone who was there. It would be virtually impossible to poison someone from afar. Of course, you could hire someone to poison a person, but even then, someone had to put the poison in the teacup, and that someone would have had to do it at the theater. She wondered out of curiosity, then, who was the crew member responsible for putting the tea in the cups.

Joan would know, of course, but just because it was someone's job to put tea in the cups—and add lemon to Joan's—didn't mean that that person necessarily also added the poison. She assumed that the cups were left sitting somewhere backstage until a crew member placed them on the little table on stage and, during that time, anyone—crew or cast—could drop poison into one of the cups. She also reasoned that everyone connected with the play probably knew that Joan's cup had the lemon slice and Belinda's cup didn't. It would be fairly easy to determine which cup would be placed before which actress. So if someone was planning to poison Belinda, it wouldn't have been difficult to slip poison directly into her cup and assume that she would drink from that cup during her scene. Of course, the killer couldn't know how much poison Belinda would consume. For all he knew, Belinda might just press her lips to the rim of the cup and pretend to sip. As it turned out, however, it appeared that the young woman did actually drink from the cup––enough to kill her. *That must have been a very concentrated dose of poison,* thought Pamela. *My recollection is that the actress just sipped a bit at that cup. I surely don't remember her gulping down any large amount.*

She ran the recording back for a third time and listened even more carefully to the pertinent—or what she considered pertinent—portions. She focused on the blackout at the end of the first scene and the beginning of the second scene. Possibly there were other segments that might provide meaningful clues, but at the moment, she placed her knowledge and experience with sound to bear on this section. The total length of the blackout, she calculated, was two minutes and fifteen seconds. The section following lasted five minutes and ten seconds from the beginning of the scene until the moment when the audience was asked to leave the theater following Belinda's collapse. That was still quite a lot of sound for analysis. Like most acoustic experts, Pamela was more typically used to analyzing segments that lasted seconds, or even milliseconds. She played the total seven minutes and twenty-five seconds over again, paying close attention to extraneous noises that she might have missed on the first playback.

The recording was definitely full of noise. It was virtually impossible to tell exactly what each noise was. Certainly if this were a video recording she would be able to look for a corresponding action on stage that would clue her to the source of a particular audio sound. As it was, she had no way of telling if a sound she heard came from the stage or the audience. This was certainly one of the drawbacks of theater-in-the-round, at least for forensics scientists. The audience was seated so close to the stage that the sounds all tended to blend together. A person coughing in the audience might sound as if they were on stage as far as the audio recorder was concerned. Pamela sighed at this dilemma until she realized that it didn't really matter to her because it didn't matter where the sound came from, only whether or not it was pertinent to discovering who killed Belinda Purvis.

Also adding to the amount of noise on the recording was the fact that the theater was housed in such an old building. With every movement that each actor took, you could almost hear the floor creak. During the performance, Pamela tended to ignore this because she was so wrapped up in the story, but now that she was concentrating on each and every noise, she realized that the Reardon Little Theater's new home upstairs of the Reardon Coffee Factory was a very squeaky, noisy place. Indeed, if the theater intended to stay in its new location, it might want to consider some noise-dampening curtains or paneling on the walls and maybe some padding under the stage floor.

She finished her third listening and rewound the recording for another go of it. Pamela was, if anything, persistent. Her ear was very sensitive and she could focus on the smallest of noises that most people would no doubt totally tune out. Hers was a world of sounds and she loved all of them—even the annoying, grating sounds of drills and lawn mowers and howling babies. *Howling babies*, she thought, remembering Arliss and her experiences as a new mother. There was one sound she didn't have to experience again.

Turning off the recorder, she leaned back in her chair and smiled.

**CHAPTER 8**

Her reverie was suddenly interrupted when a tall man, dressed in a long, wrinkled overcoat and a scarf wrapped around his neck, appeared in her doorway.

"Dr. Barnes," he greeted her with a short cough that she wasn't certain was a means to gather her attention or an actual indication of an impending cold.

"Shoop!" she responded, folding her arms and scowling. "What brings you over to my neck of the woods?" The gangly detective had been Pamela's on-again, off-again sparring partner many times in the past when she had assisted the local police in investigating various murders that had sound-related clues.

"Your buddy, Dr. Bentley," he replied with a brief bow. Scrounging around in the deep pockets of his overcoat, he drew out a large, white hanky and rubbed his nose, which was apparently dripping. "You may be aware that she was there when that young woman died the other night."

"Oh, Detective," replied Pamela, rocking back and forth in her chair as she stared at the strange man, "I'm very aware. I was there too."

"Do tell," he grumbled, eyeing her suspiciously and entering the office and plopping down on her sofa. He made no attempt to remove his coat. In fact, he pulled the collar tighter around his neck.

"You're cold, Shoop?" she asked.

"I seem to be coming down with something," he replied hoarsely. He reached in an inside pocket and drew out a red cough drop and popped it in his mouth. "You say you were there, Dr. Barnes? At the theater?" The lozenge garbled his words.

"Yes," she said. "My husband and I were in the audience. We were there in support of Joan…Dr. Bentley. It was her acting debut."

"Not a very auspicious beginning to one's career, I would think," noted the gawky man, his bushy eyebrows doing a little dance on his forehead as he peered at Pamela. "Having one of your co-actors drop dead right in the middle of the show."

"No," agreed Pamela. "A terrible thing. Are you investigating this case, Shoop?" She tapped her fingers on the edge of her desk. She had a long history with this man and, although they had worked together productively on several past investigations, he was usually annoying and seemed to relish driving her to distraction.

"Unfortunately, yes," he replied. "Our department is strapped at this time. Manpower is limited. I've got several other cases ongoing. Typically not all that many homicides in Reardon, but lately there have been quite a few. Now, this weird one."

"How weird?" she asked.

He pulled out the large, wrinkled hanky again and blew his nose loudly. *Just what I need*, thought Pamela. *Shoop's germs all over my office.*

"No motive," he said, "for one. Can't really discuss this, but then you and I have worked together so many times, Dr. Barnes, that I tend to think of you more like a colleague than a civilian."

"I don't know how to respond to that, Detective," she said, "but I guess I'm flattered. Anyway, if you're looking for Joan, you'll have to wait a while, I'm afraid. She's in class right now."

"And when will she be available?" he asked, removing a small notebook and short pencil from a pocket inside his suit coat. It was obviously difficult to balance notepad, pencil, package of cough drops, and his long scarf which was getting entangled in all of his personal items.

"Hmm," she replied, looking at her watch. "Should be maybe fifteen minutes or so."

Shoop leaned back into Pamela's couch and appeared to relax the way a sick person relaxes when they have just been tucked into a comfy bed by a solicitous nurse. He made a sad sigh. Pamela thought as she had many times before, that it was a mistake to have ever purchased that little couch for her office. It seemed to encourage visitors to remain far past their allotted time. It was one of the main reasons she spent most of her time seated there—so other people couldn't.

"Hmm," said Shoop finally, pulling his coat collar tighter around his neck. Pamela cringed. He must really be sick because it was absolutely not cold in her office. The man was no doubt experiencing chills. Maybe he even had a fever and was now spewing germs into the air. How she wished she had a spray container of disinfectant. "So, Dr. Barnes," he said, "you were there in the theater when this young woman died?"

"That's what I said," she replied. Shoop must be getting senile—or he was feverish and losing his train of thought. "Shoop, you look terrible! Why don't you go home and go to bed? Have your wife make you some chicken soup."

"Humph," he grumbled. "You saw her collapse?"

"Yes," she replied, now getting a bit testy. "I told you. I was in the audience. Rocky and I were there to support Joan. It was opening night. It was her debut!"

"Yes, debut," he repeated, coughing. "And where were you seated?"

"Shoop!" she declared. "I thought you came here to interview Joan. Are you planning on questioning every single person who was in the audience the night that poor woman died?"

"If necessary, Dr. Barnes," he said with a frown. "Truth be told, that director fellow should never have released the audience. He should have called the police and, if he had, we would have questioned everyone there before we ever allowed any audience member to leave. Someone in the audience might have seen something."

"So, you're going to go around now and try to track down everyone who was at the performance?" she asked. "There were at least a hundred, maybe two hundred people in the audience."

"One hundred and sixty," he said, correcting her. "We have some names because some of the audience members were season ticket holders and we've contacted them already. Unfortunately, some audience members just purchased tickets for the one performance and the theater has no record of those individuals." He coughed long and hard and covered his mouth with his well-used hanky.

"Maybe some of the season ticket holders will remember something," she offered with a shrug. She was actually starting to feel sorry for the man. He looked pitiful and he obviously needed medical help, but yet he was trudging ahead with his duty. She would admire this more if it weren't for the fact that he was exposing her to a possible virus.

"So far they haven't," he noted with a sound that could have been a sob. "I didn't know you and your husband had been in attendance, Dr. Barnes, because the two of you are not season ticket holders. Obviously, it comes as a delightful surprise that one of my best...uh, private contractors...you might say, was actually in attendance. It would be quite helpful if you could put your none too shabby forensic talents to work on recalling the events of the fateful night."

"The fateful night?" she asked with a chuckle. "That sounds appropriately theatrical. Shoop, you never cease to amaze me. But, in truth, I don't remember anything that could possibly help you."

"Where were you seated?" he asked ignoring her dismissal and honing in now, his infirmities set aside for the moment.

"Rocky and I were in the front row, on the right as you entered the theater. I don't know how else to describe where we were because it wasn't like a regular stage—you know, it was round and the audience sat all around it. It was strange actually. Rocky didn't like it at all. He felt like he was on display, but I found it invigorating, like I was part of the action. That is, until the actress collapsed."

"Were you close to her when that happened?" he asked.

"Actually, yes," she replied. "That little table where she was seated was almost right in front of us. During that scene, Joan was seated almost directly in front of us, and the other woman, the one who died—this

Belinda Purvis—was on the other side, further down towards our right."

"So when she collapsed," he asked, "she fell towards the center of the stage?"

"Yes," said Pamela, trying to recall the events as accurately as possible.

"Could you see her face before she fell?" asked Shoop.

"Yes," said Pamela, "very clearly. She was just a few feet away from us. I could see her sip from the tea cup and then I saw a look of, I guess, panic on her face. Then she clutched her throat and was attempting to speak. Maybe she realized what was happening and was trying to call for help."

"Did she say anything?" he asked, now leaning towards Pamela and staring at her intently.

"You mean did she produce any sound that I might recognize as an acoustics expert that possibly the average audience member wouldn't notice?"

"You could put it that way," he said. "Did she?"

"No, Detective," she said flatly.  "She made noticeable sounds. But I guarantee you that everyone in that theater recognized those sounds as the panic stricken sounds of someone who was in fear for their life.  There was simply no sound that the woman produced that my audio recorder picked up that anyone in the audience wouldn't have noticed too."

"What audio recorder?" he said abruptly.  Pamela froze. Now why did she have to go and mention that to Shoop?  The man had a way of ingratiating himself with her and getting her to relax and start chatting and then, when her guard was down, she'd go and put her foot in her mouth. Just like now.

"I, uh, recorded the production," she said sheepishly.

"You recorded it?" he asked, shocked. "Why? Did you expect the woman to die and you wanted to be prepared with a record of the happening?"

"No, of course not!" she exclaimed. "It was Joan's opening night and our friend Arliss was home with a sick child. She really wanted to be there for Joan, and Joan really wanted Arliss to be able to see her perform, so I told them both that I would record it so Arliss could hear Joan's debut. And don't ask why not a video recording. My husband and I went round and round about that. The theater won't allow video recordings of performances—for obvious reasons. They'd probably not appreciate audio recordings either, but I made one anyway."

"And you have this recording with you?" he asked. She nodded. "Does it include the actual death of Belinda Purvis?"

"Yes, it does," she said reluctantly, grabbing the little recorder from her desk. "I've actually been listening to it over and over again while I've been sitting here for the last few hours."

"And?" he asked.

"And what?" she retorted.

"Did you discover anything?" he demanded.

"Like did I do your job for you?" she countered. "No! There's really nothing of great interest on this recording."

"Nothing?" he asked.

"Nothing," she replied.

"So, then, you wouldn't mind giving it to me," he said.

"Would it matter if I did mind?" she asked.

"No," he said succinctly.  "I'd have to take it from you because it's now official evidence in an ongoing police investigation."

"Shoop," she said, rolling her desk chair around and facing him directly.  "Listen, I don't mind giving you this recording, but can you wait just a minute while I make a back-up recording?  I mean, now that I've got it, I'd like to continue listening to it and see if I can discover anything unusual about the sounds on it."

"I would insist on that," he replied.  "Make your back-up, Dr. Barnes."  She pulled an adapter cord from her middle desk drawer and attached it to both the small recorder and her computer's audio software program.  She fast forwarded the recorder to the number location where she knew the blackout began.  Hitting a few buttons, she pressed the 'play' button on the recorder and the recording began to upload into her computer software program.  When the recorder reached the point where she realized the audience had left the theater, she pressed 'stop' and detached the two devices.  Assuring herself that she had a good copy of the portion of the recording she wanted, she handed the little audio recorder to Shoop.

"There you go, Detective," she said.  "It's all yours!" She tossed him the little device which he caught with his hanky outstretched in both hands like a parachute. The man wrapped the recorder up in the cloth and shoved it into his overcoat pocket, and then, pulling his coat even tighter around his body, he pulled himself agonizingly out of Pamela's couch and headed off down the hallway, coughing and grumbling as he went. *Yikes,* she thought, *I pity the poor forensics tech who has to handle it covered with Shoop's germs.*

## CHAPTER 9

Shoop had barely disappeared down the hallway when one of Pamela's graduate students appeared at her door.  Pamela sighed with just a bit of disappointment because she was looking forward to running the audio recording through her acoustics software program. *Oh, well,* she thought. *It will just have to wait.*

She motioned Samantha Landry to enter and gave her a warm smile.  Samantha was in the last stages of her graduate program and had been struggling with writing her thesis.  In and out of her office the young woman came, day after day, as she wrote and rewrote various sections of the long manuscript, attempting to get it to meet her advisor's specifications.  Helping graduate students with their theses was a chore that Pamela usually relished.  She realized that she was good at getting her students to hone their writing— probably more so than many of her colleagues, even those who were better writers than she was.  She wasn't quite sure why this was, but she attributed it to the fact that she always made it a point to get to know each student really well and to try to understand how they thought and how they wrote.  She knew that each student worked in different ways and she encouraged them to capitalize on their strengths.

Samantha was no worse and no better than most of her students.  Pamela believed that she would finish her thesis but that it would be a struggle for her. Some students could whip out a two-hundred page thesis in a few weeks, whereas others could try and try and never really produce anything that she could approve. And it wasn't just her approval that was required. A thesis had to pass muster not just with the student's advisor, but also with their entire committee. And the committee, which included members not only from the student's home department, but also from their minor area, could often be very picky.

"Hi, Sam," she greeted the young woman, who was looking harried and ready to burst with frustration. "Hey, don't worry. It can't be that bad. We'll get it right eventually. You just need to keep plugging away..."

"No, Dr. Barnes!" exclaimed the young woman, plopping down with an audible whoosh onto the sofa. She flung her backpack beside her and clutched her kneecaps grimly. "It's not my thesis. It's worse!"

"Worse?" asked Pamela.

"I can't believe it," she said, now resting her forehead in one hand, apparently attempting to hold back a sob.

"What?" continued Pamela. "What's wrong?"

"Maybe you heard, Dr. Barnes," said the young woman in obvious distress. "About Belinda Purvis. She was murdered!"

"Yes, Sam, I did hear about that. Actually, I was there. Did you know her?"

"I did!" cried Samantha, her upper torso heaving. "She was one of my best friends. We'd been friends for years. Since elementary school."

"Oh, my god," whispered Pamela.

"I was in her wedding, Dr. Barnes," the young woman continued; her long, brown hair hung forlornly in her face, making her look less like a graduate student and more like an orphaned waif.

"Oh, dear," said Pamela, consolingly. "When was she married?"

"Just last year," sobbed Samantha. "They hadn't even been married a year, Dr. Barnes. It's so horrible! Who would want to kill Belinda?"

"Were you there, Sam?" asked Pamela delicately. "At the theater? When...all this happened?"

"No," whispered the young woman. "I wanted to go, but I had to work. I had tickets for a matinee. Belinda said that was fine. She wanted me to see her perform. She was so excited, Dr. Barnes, about being in this show! She'd never done anything like this before, but she was really loving it. And Matt, her husband. Matt Purvis. His family owns a car dealership. They've lived in Reardon for generations. He was proud of her acting too. They were just a super couple. Why would anyone want to hurt her? She was so sweet!"

"I don't know, Sam," replied Pamela. "Who knows what goes through the mind of a lunatic?"

"I'm sorry, Dr. Barnes," said Samantha, now wiping her tears and looking up directly into Pamela's face. "I shouldn't be dumping all this on you. You can probably guess that I didn't get much work done on my thesis since this all happened. All I can think about is Belinda. Why anyone would want to hurt her. Poor Matt. Oh, poor Matt." She looked down again and the tears began flowing.

"Sam, don't worry about your thesis," said Pamela, scooting her desk chair across the room and placing a hand on Samantha's arm. "That can wait. You've just suffered a terrible loss. A horrible, traumatic event and you need to deal with it. You say you and Belinda had been friends since childhood?"

"Yes," replied Samantha, looking up at Pamela, who was now clutching her hands in hers. "We used to live just a few houses from her. Our mothers were friends. They're still friends today, even though we moved to a different neighborhood."

"And you were in her wedding?"

"I was her maid of honor, Dr. Barnes!" cried Samantha, shaking her head. The young woman continued to sob uncontrollably as she spoke. "She had such a beautiful wedding. She looked amazing! It was just a perfect wedding. I have photos in my backpack." She pulled away from Pamela and grabbed her backpack, quickly unzipping it and rummaging around inside. Eventually she extracted a small cardboard folder that sported the logo of a local photography studio that Pamela recognized. "Here we are." She opened the folder to reveal a staged wedding picture of a bridal party with numerous bridesmaids and groomsmen all lined up on either side of a very attractive couple. As Pamela stared at the young man and woman in the center of the photograph, she recognized Belinda Purvis, now in a long, full chiffon wedding dress, not a turn of the century gown such as she had worn in 'The Importance of Being Earnest.' Her hair was fixed differently but it was still the young woman who had died violently before her eyes just a few days ago.

It gave Pamela chills to look at this photograph and see this young victim in such a happy moment. After staring at Belinda Purvis, her eyes moved over to the left of the bride where she saw the happy face of the young woman sitting beside her on the sofa. Then, her eyes continued to the right and she saw the handsome countenance of Belinda's husband, Matt Purvis. As she examined his face, she realized that she recognized him too. He had been the man in the audience sitting across from them during the performance—the one who had leaped forward onto the stage when Belinda Purvis had collapsed.

"I saw the husband at the performance," noted Pamela to Samantha as they both looked at the wedding photo. He was there in the audience."

"Yes," said Samantha. "Matt was excited about Belinda's show. He was really proud of her! They were so much in love. He just must be brokenhearted." Samantha slowly folded up the wedding picture and placed it carefully back in her backpack.

"Had she known her husband for a long time?" asked Pamela, attempting to make conversation. Sometimes, she'd realized people who were in pain needed to talk about the painful experience.

"Yes," said Samantha, "almost as long as she'd known me. The Purvises and the Whatleys are long-time residents of Reardon, Dr. Barnes. They go way back. I don't know if they founded the town or anything like that, but both families are important in the community." She'd said *important* as if she'd meant *socially prominent* or at least that's how Pamela interpreted her comment.

"Can you think of any reason that anyone would have to harm Belinda?" asked Pamela.

"No," she said defiantly. "Do you think that someone did this intentionally, Dr. Barnes?"

Pamela hesitated because she realized that it was difficult enough to have someone you love die, but to think that someone, anyone, had a rational reason for wanting that person dead...that might just be too much for anyone to consider.

"I don't know what the police are thinking right now, Samantha," said Pamela, "but she was poisoned. That was revealed in the autopsy report which was on television the other night.  That wasn't an accident. Someone did this intentionally."

"I just can't believe that anyone would do this to Belinda," said Samantha insistently.  "She wouldn't hurt a flea."

"Maybe not," said Pamela carefully, "but it doesn't appear that anyone else was targeted.  The killer apparently was aiming for Belinda."

"No," insisted Samantha. "It doesn't make sense. It must be a mistake.  Maybe the person...the killer...just hates everyone and just put that poison in there and didn't really care who he killed.  Belinda just happened to be the victim."

"It's possible," agreed Pamela, "but unlikely.  It appears that the killer specifically targeted the cup that Belinda used—not the cup that the other actress used. I know this because the other actress is Dr. Bentley."

"Oh, yes," said Samantha. "Belinda told me that Dr. Bentley was playing her mother.  She was so excited about that.  She'd taken a class in our department, Dr. Barnes, before she graduated and so she'd heard of Dr. Bentley.  I mean, all the students at Grace have heard of Dr. Bentley, no matter what department they're in. Belinda said she was so nice and so much fun!"

*A fairly ringing endorsement of my friend*, thought Pamela.  Of course, she knew that Joan wasn't all that interested in the female cast members, but even so, knowing Joan, she knew that her friend would have been courteous to all of the cast members—no matter their sex.

"That's nice to know, Samantha," said Pamela, tucking away that little tidbit to give to Joan later. "However, because I was there at the performance and because Dr. Bentley was there too, we're possibly more aware of what's happening with the police investigation..."

"Oh, and because you help the police, Dr. Barnes!" exclaimed Samantha. "I've heard that you have sometimes helped the police solve murders. I believe someone said that it was you who solved the murder of that famous professor, that Dr. Clark, a few years ago."

"Oh, I may have assisted a bit," said Pamela, "but nothing much." She didn't want this conversation to focus on her.

"Maybe you can help find out who killed Belinda, Dr. Barnes!" Samantha shouted suddenly, sitting up straight on the sofa and turning directly to face her advisor.

"Oh no," said Pamela with a sigh. "It's not really..." The last thing she needed was her students egging her on to get involved in this murder case.

"Please, Dr. Barnes!" continued Samantha.

Pamela sighed and, patting Samantha's hands, she rose from the sofa. "Samantha, let's just wait and see. If the police really need any of my skills, you know I'll do what I can. But right now, my main concern is you and helping you cope with the loss of your friend. And my order to you is not to fret over working on your thesis for a while. Just concentrate on dealing with your own grief—and helping your family and friends deal with theirs.  Okay?"

"Okay," replied the young woman who then gathered her backpack and stood up.  Pamela gave her a warm hug and the young woman headed out of the office.

## CHAPTER 10

That night Rocky prepared some easy to eat finger food for the two of them to munch on while watching the local news.  They were on their bed, nibbling on crudités and some of Rocky's cheesy ham and egg muffins, with Candide banished to the floor while they dined.  Undaunted, the fluffy little dog stood at attention at the foot of the bed, hoping that one of his owners would take pity and fling him a tasty treat.

"Shoo, Candide!" said Rocky, as Candide made his wishes known with some well-placed, high-pitched poodle barks.  "This is people food."

"He prefers people food," said Pamela, ignoring her husband's admonition and dropping a tiny bit of egg muffin on the floor where the puppy retrieved it and quickly nibbled down the morsel.

"Now you've started something," said Rocky. "You'll never get rid of him and we'll never be able to hear the news."

"You made enough of these little things to feed an army," she noted as she slathered butter on her second muffin.  "Umm, they're good though.  No doubt, horribly fattening.  I'll just give Candide a whole one and that'll keep him busy."

"I doubt it," replied Rocky with a scowl.  "These are not doggie treats.  And they're only fattening if you cover them in butter."

"Oh, come on, Rocky," she said, dropping the knife back into the tub of butter set between them. "Candide just appreciates your culinary skills as much as I do!" She gave him a cheesy grin, butter dripping down her chin as she popped a third little muffin into her mouth.

"You seem to like those," he said.

"Yum," she replied between bites. "Good." She pulled off another piece of muffin and tossed it to Candide, who caught it mid-air and gobbled it whole, then disappeared under an armchair with his treasure.

Before Rocky could argue with her tactics any further, the local news anchor announced an upcoming story about the recent murder of a local actress. She thought it was unusual that they were labeling Belinda Purvis an "actress" when she'd never actually completed her first acting role. However, she focused her attention as the scene on the television screen changed to a reporter standing in front of what she recognized as Reardon's county court house. She knew that this large, two-story building housed all of the civic offices—including Shoop's, a place she had visited more than once. The reporter spoke into the camera.

"Sharon," said the young woman with the microphone, "the Coroner's Office has just released new information regarding its findings from the autopsy of Belinda Purvis, the young woman who was murdered last weekend at the Reardon Community Theater's opening night performance of 'The Importance of Being Earnest.'"

"Eve, have they determined anything about the poison used to kill Ms. Purvis?" asked the anchor back in the studio. The screen changed to show the local anchor as she asked this question, then immediately returned to the remote reporter at the court house.

"Yes," replied Eve, the reporter, "we've learned from sources in the coroner's office that it does appear that Ms. Purvis was poisoned. She apparently had not eaten for at least twelve hours before her death, as determined from her stomach contents. They're still waiting for their initial findings to be confirmed by further toxicology tests, but it's looking more and more as if Belinda Purvis died from ingesting a poison that was dissolved in a liquid that she drank immediately before she died. The police indicate that Ms. Purvis drank from a cup on stage shortly before her death. Another actress sitting next to Ms. Purvis was unharmed."

"They mean Joan," said Pamela, nudging Rocky.

"The police have stated that it appears that Ms. Purvis was the target of this murder and that no other individual was in danger from the poison."

"Do the police have any idea what the motive might be for this crime, Eve?" asked the anchorwoman.

"Not yet," replied Eve, looking directly into the camera. "They are questioning all members of the cast and crew of the production, and are also attempting to question audience members who witnessed the crime. Apparently, Sharon, the audience was dismissed shortly after Ms. Purvis collapsed on stage but before the police arrived. I have been told by a...Detective Shoop...who, I believe, is the lead investigator..."

"Oh, no!" cried Rocky. "Shoop! Just what they need." Rocky had had his own run-ins with Shoop and, although Shoop apparently was sympathetic with Pamela's husband, Rocky did not return the feeling.

"I've been told," the reporter continued, "that anyone who was in attendance at the production and witnessed the death of Ms. Purvis should contact the Reardon Police Department.  They would like to question each and every audience member in the hopes that one or more of them might remember something that might prove valuable to the investigation."

"Thank you, Eve, for updating us," said the anchor. "We'll look forward to hearing any new information you bring us."  With that, the scene changed and the anchor moved on to a different local story.

"So, Shoop is leading this investigation," noted Rocky, shaking his head.  "He really seems to get his nose in everything.  Don't they have any other detectives?"

"I don't know, Rocky," replied Pamela, leaning back in her bed, satiated from her dinner.  "He didn't say."

"What do you mean, *he* didn't say?" he asked in an accusatory manner, moving up and leaning in to her. "When did you talk to him?"

"Umm, this afternoon," she said, cringing.  "He just dropped by, looking for Joan.  You know, because she was in the show.  He wanted to question her some more about Belinda's death."

"And, of course, when he gets together with you— his old buddy—he just can't pull himself away, and the two of you have to talk shop!?"  Rocky growled.

"We do have a sort of history," she replied.  "You know, we've worked together successfully to solve a number of cases.   It's not unusual that he might...confide in me, is it?"

"Humph," snorted her husband.   "So, did he? Confide in you, I mean."

"Not really," she said.  "It was more like he was questioning me—you know, when he discovered that we were there when the murder took place.  He figured I might have noticed something that some other audience member didn't."

"And?"  Rocky crossed his arms and gave her that annoyed husband look of his.

"I just told him that I'd made that audio recording for Arliss and he asked me for it," she said with a shrug.

"You gave it to him?"

"I did," she said.

"Good," he pronounced with a firm nod.  "Now, maybe that will be that."

"Of course, I did make a copy first," she added flippantly.  "I mean, he didn't mind.  He even waited while I uploaded the pertinent segment onto my computer."

"The pertinent segment?" he cried.  "What do you mean by that?"

"The part where...where," she stammered, "where, you know, where the poisoning might have, probably did take place."

"And where would that be, madam prosecutor?" he asked with a smile.  "You know exactly when this killer placed the poison?  How would that be?"

"I don't know, Rocky," she whined.  "But it had to be sometime during the show.  You heard that reporter just say so on the news!  Maybe there's some evidence on my audio recording that will indicate who poisoned Belinda Purvis—and how, and when!"

Rocky sighed and drew up his knees to his chest, shaking his head.  "I cannot get a break," he declared.  "It just doesn't appear that any murder that occurs in this town can go unnoticed by my wife, the detective! You always seem to have some reason to get involved!"

"Rocky!" she cried. "I'm not involved. I just gave the recording to Shoop. How he uses it is his business."

"But he knows you have a copy," continued an irate Rocky. "You know he'll expect you to analyze that recording and look for some acoustic clue that he won't be able to find. You know it, Pamela!"

"I don't know any such thing!" she shouted. The loud voices awakened Candide who crawled out from under the blue armchair across the bedroom. The little dog moseyed over to Pamela's side of the bed and rose up on his hind legs and started scratching pitifully on the bedspread. "Now, we've disturbed Candide and he wants our attention."

"We've finished the food," said Rocky. He held up his arms to indicate that there was nothing more their pet could want. Pamela lifted Candide up onto the bed and plopped him down between them.

"Okay, you little diplomat," she said. "Can you help us solve our marital problems?" Candide licked her face joyfully and then bounded across her stomach and licked Rocky's face too.

"It's probably all the salt and butter left over from those muffins," he noted.

"No," she said. "He loves us. He doesn't like it when we fight. He's our little tiny marriage counselor." She picked up the dog and squeezed him warmly. Rocky reached over and tousled the creature's furry head.

"Okay, buddy," he said to Candide, "you are a good little mediator." The petting and snuggling continued with all three participants enjoying the outpouring of affection. It was unclear who benefited the most—Pamela, Rocky, or Candide. Eventually, the couple fell asleep and Candide joyfully settled down for a very special nap between his two favorite humans. For the moment, at least, there was no thought at all about Belinda Purvis and who might have murdered her.

## CHAPTER 11

She was sitting with her nose almost touching her computer screen as her eyes focused on the fluctuating lines of the acoustic signals while the murder recording played out visually across her monitor.  She'd watched this section several times now, the conglomeration of noises during the blackout creating a strange pattern of spiky lines and troughs on the screen before her.  Her experienced eye strove to find some semblance of meaning in one or any of the lines.  Could she recognize one of these squiggly marks as an indication of a killer placing poison in a cup?  Or was this a wild goose chase?  The foul deed had probably been accomplished backstage long before her little audio recording started to pick up the sounds of the production.

She'd looked at the screen for so long in this frozen position that she'd developed a kink in her neck.  She leaned back in her desk chair and reached up to rub the offending spot.  Just at that moment her colleague and office neighbor, Willard Swinton, came into view.  She should have heard him coming around the hallway as Willard was one of the department's elder professors and used a cane to get around.  As it was, he was probably one of the youngest spirits she knew, even if his large, slow-moving body appeared to be fighting his energetic mind at every turn.

"Pamela," he sang out as he greeted her with a cheerful entrance wave.

"Willard!" she responded. "Come in! You're a pleasant relief from staring at this screen. I think I'm getting eye strain." She rubbed her eyes and motioned for him to enter and take the sofa. Willard hobbled carefully over to the couch and cautiously lowered himself to the soft cushions. His cheerful face belied the obvious pain involved in any sort of extreme movement—such as sitting down.

"My goodness!" he said with a sort of whistle, "that couch gets lower every time I sit in it!" He laughed and she joined in. She was more than concerned for Willard—not so concerned that she would ever suggest that he consider retiring. Their relationship was simply not that intimate. However, their professional relationship was about as tight as any in the department. They had collaborated on numerous research projects and several of their scholarly papers had been published. More recently, Willard had willingly—some might say, joyfully—assisted Pamela in investigating the forensic nature of several murders.

"How are you?" she asked, foregoing her forensic questions as she stared at the round, almost cherubic face of her friend. "Are you sure you should be walking around...like...?"

"Like a fat, old professor with major hip problems?" he finished for her, chuckling. "Don't you fret over me, Pamela. I'm not going to let my mobility—or lack of it—stand in my way."

"I'm just concerned, Willard," said Pamela sincerely. "You really seem to be struggling."

"The best medicine for sore joints," he said with a shake of his stubby, brown finger, "is a good mystery. And word has it that you've got yourself a new one."

"I guess I do," she replied with a shrug. "So, if you need drugs, I've got a veritable medicine chest full."

"Do tell, my dear," he replied gleefully, placing his ivory-handled cane on the side of Pamela's couch and leaning forward. "What is the crime? Possibly the death of that young woman in that play the other night?"

"Now what made you think that, Willard?" she asked him with a devilish grin. "Have you been talking to Joan?"

"Our dear friend Dr. Bentley may have mentioned something about being in a dramatic performance," he said with a flourish of his hands and a cheesy smile. "That or the large poster for the production taped prominently to her office door."

"Yes, certainly," she said. "She probably bent your ear for an hour telling you how wonderful she was—or would have been—if it hadn't been for the unfortunate death of her cast mate."

"A terrible tragedy," he said. "A very young woman. Word has it she'd taken a class or two in our department."

"So that makes us responsible to track down her killer?" asked Pamela.

"No, of course not," replied Willard sincerely, "but I figured that if anyone here in Psychology could do anything it would be you, Pamela."

"You flatter me, Willard," replied Pamela. "I doubt if there's anything I can do. However, if there is, you know I will do what I can."

"As will I," said the older man. "So?"

"So?" she repeated.

"So," he continued.  "What are your clues?  I assume you have something you're working on.  You aren't all bent out of shape leaning over your monitor because of some new experiment, at least not one you're working on with me.  Come, come now.  Out with it."

"All right, Willard," she replied.  "It's no secret.  It's really an accident."

"An accident?"

"Yes, you see, I happened to be at that performance where that young woman was killed the other night.  I was there for Joan.  Arliss was supposed to be there too, but her baby was sick and she couldn't attend, so I promised her I'd record the show for her."

"Very thoughtful," he said, nodding, "and I see where this is going."

"I figured you would," she said.  "Anyway, I made an audio recording of the production and then forgot about it during all the excitement when the young woman collapsed on stage.  It wasn't until later that we learned that she'd been murdered and I started to think about this recording.  And then, the other day, Shoop—you remember him?  That detective whom I worked with before when I helped with those other cases?"

"Oh, yes!" he said with excitement.  "Does this Shoop, this detective, want you to investigate this case too?"

"He actually just wanted the audio recording," she said.  "So I gave it to him.  But not before I made a copy to analyze myself."

"Wise woman," he said, nodding.  "So?"

"So?" she retorted.

"What have you discovered?" he demanded cheerfully. "You say you're sore from staring at your screen. I assume you've been staring at the acoustic output from this audio recording of the murder?"

"Yes," she sighed, "but I can't really see anything. There's so much noise going on, I can't really even isolate any of the acoustic signals for any of the sounds."

"Maybe I can help?" he offered.

"Would you?"

"The hard part will be just getting over to your computer," he said, grabbing his cane and balancing it between his legs and slowly pushing himself up. His effort, punctuated with huffing and puffing, was eventually rewarded by an upright position. Pamela had, in the meantime, pulled the straight back chair near her doorway to beside her. Willard waddled over and carefully placed his giant form into the tiny seat.

"I'll play the whole thing for you," she said, quickly placing her cursor at the beginning of the audio segment on the screen. "This is the beginning of the blackout. I just saved this segment because I believe that if the killer does actually attempt to place the poison on stage it would have to occur during this portion of time. This runs from the beginning of the blackout at the end of the first scene, through the beginning of the second scene and up until Belinda Purvis drinks from the teacup in front of her, and then collapses. My original recording ran much longer— until Rocky and I returned home and I eventually remembered that I had the recording still running— but I only saved this short segment, where I think the actual poisoning must have occurred. The whole thing runs a few minutes." She hit 'play' and sound emitted from the speakers on the side of her monitor.

Willard listened closely as did Pamela, their two faces staring straight ahead at the opposite wall. After a few minutes, as Pamela had predicted, the recording ended with the entrance of the director, Ron Whitcomb, who sent the audience home.

"My goodness," said Willard, turning to Pamela seated next to him. "There is certainly a lot of sound all going on at once during that blackout. The music only covers the noise of scuffling and tinkling."

"Yes," agreed Pamela, "obviously, that's the intent. They want the audience to focus on the music and not be distracted by the crew members moving things around on stage."

"Do you think we could figure out what the various noises are?" he asked with glee.

"I think we have to," she said quickly, "if we're ever going to determine if any of those noises represent a sound or sounds made by our killer. It's unlikely the killer was onstage during the blackout. Don't you think?"

"Hmm," he said, "definitely. Let's hear it again." He placed his chin on the top of his cane handle in a sort of ready position. Pamela pressed the button and the same recording arose again through the speakers.

At the end of the second playing, Willard commented, "The music is definitely louder than the ambient noises."

"That's obviously what they wanted," she said. "Nobody wants to just sit in a dark theater and listen to the sounds of furniture being moved or props being changed around."

"Too bad," he said. "For us, anyway."

"Yes, too bad."

"But, of course, very good that you recorded this, my dear!" he added when her face appeared to droop. "You were definitely Johnny on the spot in this case."

"It wasn't planned, Willard," she said.  "Just fortuitous circumstances."

"Yes, yes," he agreed.  "Now, play it again, my dear."  She complied and for a third time, the two professors sat and listened and watched intently as the sounds and acoustic output repeated.

At the end of the replay, Willard leaned back and sucked on his lower lip, apparently in thought.

"What does Joan say about all of this, Pamela?" he asked.

"You mean the murder?"

"Yes," he said.  "She must be horrified.  I mean she was sitting right across from the young woman who died."

"Yes," agreed Pamela.  "It must have been terrible for her.  I know it was awful for me and I didn't know her at all, but she was just a few feet in front of me. We were in the front row.  We could see everything."

"Ghastly," said Willard.  "Of course, knowing Joan, she's probably equally concerned about the postponement of the production?" he asked cautiously.

"You know our Joan well, Willard," said Pamela with one raised eyebrow.  "I don't mean to be disparaging towards her, but let's just say she's very anxious for the show to go on—as they say in theater talk."

"Yes, the show must go on!" he said in a soft whisper and did a little fist pump.  Pamela chuckled.

"I remember thinking the night of the show that they really rehearsed their set changes well.  I don't know what they did, but it was really quick and really quiet."

"Must have been practiced," he said. "I'm guessing they probably practice set changes as much as they practice the show."

"That they did," she said, "according to Joan, at least. She said their director, this Ron Whitcomb, was a stickler for precision."

"Maybe he would recognize the sounds during the blackout," suggested Willard.

"Maybe," she said, "let's worry about that later, though. Right now, I'm more concerned about determining what we can from the acoustic signature."

"I'm with you there, my dear," he agreed and the two peered intently at the frozen image of spiked lines on the screen.

"Does anything look particularly unusual to you?" she asked.

"Not really," he responded.

"Just how much sound would a person make who decided to place poison in the cup of an actress during a well-practiced blackout?" she speculated.

"If, indeed, that's when the killer put the poison in the cup," he added.

"Indeed."

## CHAPTER 12

Unfortunately, all of their efforts were to no avail and eventually Willard returned to his office. This was what Pamela was contemplating—his sort of sad retreat down the hallway—as she sipped her margarita. She was alone in her favorite booth at *WhoWho's* cantina awaiting the arrival of Joan and Arliss for their regular Friday night girls' outing. Right on cue, the two friends poured into the seats beside her, already embroiled in conversation which sounded almost like argument.

"Baby, baby!" cried Joan, as she flung her purse on the seat and leaned back in the booth. Arliss scooted in beside Pamela. "Is that all you talk about?"

"He's been sick, Joan!" scowled Arliss, her elbows planted firmly on the wooden table before her.

"Really, Joan," admonished Pamela, without taking her lips from the rim of the cocktail glass.

A pert waiter appeared with order pad primed at the ready. His festive orange and yellow shirt matched the cheerful decor of the little restaurant. A lively Mexican band was playing—possibly live somewhere further back in the restaurant, but more likely recorded.

"Our usual, Fernando," said Joan with a wave of her hand as she extricated herself from her stylish suede jacket.

Fernando said, "Two more margaritas for the three lovely ladies?" and Arliss and Joan both nodded and vocally affirmed their order. The waiter disappeared without a sound.

"Don't tell me Noah is sick again?" asked Pamela with concern, turning to Arliss seated close beside her in the small booth. Arliss looked more disheveled than usual. Her hair was hanging limply around her face, her rubber band barely maintaining the massive bulk of her hair in a loose bundle atop her head.

"No," replied her lanky friend, leaning back and pulling up a leg onto the seat. Pamela leaned back into the corner and gave her friend some room to stretch out. "He's definitely better, but we're keeping an eye on him. You know babies!" Pamela thought she detected a bit of drool staining the front of Arliss's regular formless white shirt.

"I do," replied Pamela. "Or at least, I did once upon a time." She smiled at Arliss and turned to Joan who gave her a pronounced grimace and threw up her hands.

"Really, Arliss!" added Joan, rolling her eyes. "You were never this attentive to those lab critters of yours when they got the sniffles!"

"Joan!" cried Pamela. "Noah is not a critter! He's a human being. You should be more understanding."

"Oh, don't worry, Pam," said Arliss with a wave of her hand. "I understand exactly where Joan is coming from. I probably am overreacting way too much. I really don't have anyone to model myself on; my own mother was rather hands off. I guess that's why I always spent so much time with animals—they satisfied my motherly instincts."

"And now you have a real baby to expend those instincts on, Arliss," said Pamela, "and it's perfectly understandable that you're concerned."

"Doting," said Joan.

"I'm here," replied Arliss to her friend across the table. She rolled her leg around, tucked it under the booth bench, and leaned over the table and pointed her finger at Joan. "And believe me, I'm anxious for some adult conversation. So, talk, Joan!"

"Yes, Joan," added Pamela, bending in beside Arliss, their two heads almost joined at the ears. "You have an audience, so talk!"

"Humph!" snorted Joan, now apparently satisfied that she had their attention. "That's more like it. I'd hate to see our regular Friday girls' nights out turned into some mommy play date."

"No fear of that," noted Pamela, "as my only child is an adult, as are your two boys. Right?"

"They are," said Joan with a smile.

"Believe me," said Arliss, looking back and forth from one friend to another, "I've been longing for this night for days now. I haven't seen either of you since all of that excitement with your play, Joan. What's been going on? Have they discovered who killed that poor girl yet?" She pushed a large, wayward clump of hair behind her ear.

"No," replied Joan. "Although I'm sure Pamela can provide more information than I can on the investigation."

"What?" asked Arliss. "Pamela, you're not involved in this case too, are you?" Both Arliss and Joan had direct knowledge of her past investigations. They'd even participated in some of them.

"What are you talking about, Joan?" asked Pamela.

"Oh, don't play coy with me, girl," said Joan, chastising her friend across the table.  "I know what you're up to.  Your old buddy Shoop let it slip that you were assisting him on this case when he came by my office the other day to ask me some more questions."

"Shoop is the lead investigator on this one?" asked Arliss, who knew as well as Joan did the close working relationship that their friend had shared with the strange police officer.

"Yes," replied Pamela.

"So, just how did he rope you into helping him again?" asked Joan, gulping the last of her margarita and waving her empty glass around until Fernando appeared out of nowhere and took the glass and almost as promptly returned with another.

"You downed that one really fast, Joan," noted Arliss.

"You drove," replied the older woman, flipping her hair with a little flirtatious shake of her shoulders.

"I'm not going to pour you into my car like I did the last time," pouted Arliss.

"Oh, don't be such a party pooper, Arliss," said Joan.  "Ever since you had that baby, you've become such a goodie two-shoes."

"At least I can stand up in my shoes when I go drinking," replied Arliss with a huff.  Joan ignored her and took another big gulp of her second margarita. Arliss and Pamela glanced at each other with worried looks as they discreetly sipped on their first drinks.

"Joan," interjected Pamela, in an obvious attempt to focus Joan's attention on something other than alcohol.  "What else did Shoop ask you about when he came by your office the other day?"

"Oh, not much!" Joan replied with a dramatic wave of her free hand. "He kept going over where I was at different times during the performance. He wanted to know where I was standing, what I'd seen, what props I'd touched or moved. And, of course, if I'd seen anybody else touching or moving any of the props."

"Do you think they have any idea who might have poisoned that actress?" asked Arliss.

"You mean Belinda," said Joan.

"Yes," said Arliss. "Joan, you were there. You saw what was going on, on stage and off stage. Did you notice anything unusual?"

"No," said Joan, "and I told that to Shoop too. Ron, the director, runs...ran a tight ship. That was something I appreciated. He is—was organized and that play moved along like clockwork. You may have noticed, Pamela, that the set changes were very quick and efficient—at least the one you experienced."

"It was," agreed Pamela. "It seemed as if people were moving about in the dark as if they knew exactly what they had to do and where they needed to go. Truthfully, I was amazed that no one bumped into each other."

"Oh, they did at first!" exclaimed Joan. "When we practiced it the first few times. But Ron always said that the set changes were just as important as the play itself and he made us go over and over them, so that they were short and noiseless."

"Of course," added Pamela, "you did have that music playing. I guess that was to cover up any noise made during the set change."

"Yes," said Joan, "and to give the audience something to focus on other than the rather boring sounds of people moving things around."

"So," said Arliss, "let me get this straight.  You practiced the set changes."

"And timed them," added Joan.  "Ron would sit there with a stop watch and call out the seconds as we did the changes.  He expected us to get them shorter and shorter each time and we had to repeat them over and over until he was satisfied that they were short enough."

"Goodness!" said Pamela.  "That's impressive.  So, each crew member had a specific job to perform."

"Actually," said Joan.  "Each actor had a specific job. We really don't—didn't—have many crew members. Just a stage manager and a costume director.  The stage manager announced the blackout and then each actor had a job to perform."

"So, you were a crew member as well as an actor," noted Arliss, still sipping her margarita very slowly.

"I was," explained Joan, having slowed her own intake of beverage a bit.  The second margarita was taking her definitely more time than the first.  "My job during the first blackout was to move the suitcase from in front of the bench to beside the far entrance.  It was quite easy to do and I just zipped over there and did it and then exited."

"Do you know what jobs the other actors had during the blackout?" asked Pamela, looking down into her half-full glass.

"I can't remember what everyone did in every blackout, Pamela," said Joan, setting down her glass with obvious annoyance.  "It was only my job to remember my own duties, which I did."

"I can imagine the police will want to know who was responsible for putting the teapot and tea cups on the little table," mused Pamela as she took another sip of her margarita.

"Oh, that!" said Joan with a flourish. "That was Belinda's job. She went offstage during the blackout, grabbed the tea tray with the pot and cups, set it on the table and then placed the cups before the appropriate spots."

"You mean she was the one who placed the cup with the poison in it that killed her on the table?" asked Arliss.

"I guess she did," replied Joan, furrowing her brow as she attempted to remember the sequence of events.

"Just think, Joan," said Arliss in a hushed voice, "if Belinda had put the poisoned cup in front of you instead of in front of herself, you would have drunk it and..."

"Which seems to prove," added Pamela, attempting to defer the obvious horrific direction of this train of thought, "that Belinda had no idea that there was poison in the cup that was intended for her."

"And how did she know which cup was intended for her?" asked Arliss.

"Because of the lemon," said Pamela quickly.

"Oh, yes!" cried Arliss. "I remember! That's how you said they placed the cups on the table—yours with the lemon slice and Belinda's without. You just didn't say that Belinda was the one who set it up that way after the blackout."

"She was the one who did it after the first blackout," noted Joan. "In some of the later set changes, other people did it. But, of course, no one ever saw those because the performance never got farther than the first set change on opening night."

"And Shoop knows all this?" asked Pamela. "About the lemon? About Belinda setting the cups and tea pot during the first blackout?"

"Yes, yes," said an annoyed Joan, "he knows!"

"My goodness, Pamela," said Arliss, flipping her frizzy black hair towards Pamela so quickly that Pamela felt that some of it might float away, "what will the police think now? I mean, the person who set the cups and tea pot would be the prime suspect. But, if the victim—Belinda—is the person who set the poisoned cup right in front of her own place, Shoop can't possibly suspect her. Can he?"

"Of course not," replied Joan and Pamela at almost the same time. Joan took a sip of her drink and gestured for Pamela to continue.

"No, it certainly looks as if the killer put that poison in the cup before the blackout when it was backstage. It looks as if Belinda had no idea she was sealing her own doom when she set the cups on the table during the blackout. Wouldn't you agree, Joan?"

"Yes, of course," said Joan.

"It's just lucky," added Arliss, "that she didn't accidentally switch the two cups." She looked up at Joan forlornly and Joan gave a little whimper. At that moment, Arliss's phone rang. She answered it, only to discover that baby Noah had spiked another fever. Arliss left abruptly, leaving Pamela to take the somewhat inebriated Joan home.

**CHAPTER 13**

Rocky had become accustomed to his wife's Friday night forays with her two friends so when she returned late Friday night, he merely guided her inside and helped her into bed without much conversation.  It was so late that Candide was even too tired to greet her at the door when she returned.  The couple was soon sound asleep when the front doorbell rang.

"Oh, no!" cried Pamela, sitting bolt upright in bed.  "Who can that be?"

Rocky rolled over on his side of the bed and peered at his alarm clock from one sleepy eye.  "It's midnight!  Good grief!"  As Pamela sat with the covers clutched around her, Rocky climbed out of bed, grabbing a bathrobe on his way to the front door.

"Don't answer it!" she admonished him.  "It might be a prank.  Just peek through the hole in the door!"

"Don't worry!" he called back in a loud whisper.  Not able to contain her curiosity and concern over their late night caller, Pamela got out of bed too and put on her robe and slippers which she kept on a chair near the bed.  She tip-toed into the living room at a discreet distance behind her husband.  She could see him at the door, his eye to the small opening.  The door bell sounded again.

"What the...?" cried Rocky, turning back to her with a grimace.  He opened the door.

"Rocky!" she cried.  "Don't!  Who is it?"  She clutched her robe tightly around her body as she clung to the edge of a dining room chair.

"Detective," said Rocky to the visitor whom Pamela couldn't see from her vantage point.  Pamela could hear a voice she recognized but couldn't make out what was being said.  She quickly joined Rocky at the front door.  Standing on her front porch was her nemesis, Shoop, accompanied by a uniformed officer.

"What's wrong?" she asked him.

"He wants to question us," replied Rocky, turning to Pamela.

"What?!" she cried.  "It's the middle of the night!"

"Actually, Dr. Barnes," said Shoop, lifting his watch and glancing at it, "it's not quite midnight.  I assumed you would be awake.  It is Friday and, if my memory serves me right, you do have a standing date with your female cohorts at the local watering hole, don't you?  One of my officers noticed you driving down the highway rather slowly—and a bit irratically.  He thought about pulling you over, but called me instead.  I figured I'd just catch you about the time you were returning from your wild gallivanting."  He stared at her expressionless as his eyes moved from her head to her feet.  "Evidently, I missed my mark by a few hours.  I guess you're not the party girl I thought you were."

"I am too!" cried Pamela, now squeezing her robe more tightly, "I mean, Shoop, it's none of your business what sort of party girl I am.  I mean, I'm not a party girl.  I mean..."

"I need to ask you and your husband a few questions," he continued.

"We were asleep," said Rocky.  "Can't this wait until tomorrow?"  He yawned pronouncedly.

"It will only take a few minutes," said Shoop, undaunted by the sight of Pamela and Rocky standing before him in their pajamas. "Officer Ryan and I have come out here and we'd really appreciate just a few minutes of your time." He looked from Pamela to Rocky and gave each a beaming smile. Officer Ryan remained stone-faced.

"Oh, for heaven's sake!" said Pamela, with a pitiful glance at Rocky, "just a few minutes!" Rocky snarled noticeably at her, but moved aside just the same as Shoop entered their home and trudged into their living room, followed by the officer. Pamela followed them and Rocky traipsed along behind her.

"Why don't we sit?" suggested Shoop, with a gesture to his hosts that would have been more appropriate coming from them. Pamela and Rocky carefully sat together on their sofa and Shoop alighted on an armchair across from them. Officer Ryan remained standing near the entrance.

"All right, Shoop," said Pamela wearily, "just what is so important that you had to wake us up in the middle of the night?"

"Dr. Barnes," began Shoop, extracting his small notebook and pencil from inside his overcoat pocket, "I have your statement about the events that you remember the night Ms. Purvis died, but you told us that your husband was also in the audience. I need to ask you, Mr. Barnes, your recollection of the performance. If you remember anything that possibly you wife doesn't."

"That's it?" asked Pamela. "You couldn't ask him that during the daytime?"

"We happened to be in the neighborhood," replied Shoop. "Can you tell us what you remember, sir?"

"It's okay, Pammie," said Rocky with a sigh. "Let's just get this over with. You know I'm going to have to give my statement sooner or later. Now that we're up, I might as well do it now. It's better than having to go down to the police station."

"A very sensible attitude, Mr. Barnes," said Shoop with a small smile. He poised his pencil over his little notebook.

The voices had evidently awakened Candide, who wandered into the living room from his favorite sleeping spot under the couple's bed. The little dog perked up immediately when he saw two strangers in his domain and immediately went into guard dog mode, yapping and leaping up on Officer Ryan's leg.

"Candide!" yelled Rocky, "Down! Down!" Candide reluctantly responded to Rocky's command, but not without eyeing the two strangers who were invading his turf at a most indecent hour. He took up a watchful position about a foot from the officer, apparently ready to pounce whenever his master gave the command.

"Quite a dangerous dog you have there," noted Shoop. Candide's little pink tongue hung out as he panted in repressed excitement. The poodle suddenly opened his mouth wide and displayed a tiny row of teeth.

"Yes, Shoop," replied Pamela. "He'll protect us to the death and don't you forget it!" She frowned at the detective and pulled the collar of her robe up around her ears. "Good boy, Candide!"

"Anyway, you were saying, Mr. Barnes," said Shoop, gesturing to Rocky to continue with his narration.

"I don't know what Pamela has already told you," he said.

"It doesn't matter," replied Shoop.  "We want to hear your recollection.   Just tell us what you remember."

Rocky took a deep breath, glancing from his wife to the tall detective who was bunched up in his wrinkled overcoat in a big lump in their living room arm chair.  "I really wasn't paying a lot of attention.  I sort of got dragged to this show."  He looked briefly at Pamela and she rolled her eyes at him.  Shoop noted their interaction and quickly jotted something in his little book.

"Don't we all, Mr. Barnes, don't we all."  He shook his head forlornly and nibbled on the tip of his pencil.

"Actually my wife's friend was supposed to be there, but her baby got sick at the last minute," he said.

"Or so she said," added Shoop, with a conspiratorial wink at Rocky.

"Yeah," replied Rocky.  "You're probably right.  A clever ploy to get out of sitting through..."

"Rocky!" cried Pamela.

"Sorry," Rocky replied sheepishly.

"Go on, Mr. Barnes," said Shoop, quickly intervening between the couple.

"Anyway," continued Rocky, "I was there.  We were there...in the front row.  It was quite uncomfortable, I thought, because it was right on the edge of the performing area.  You could almost reach out and touch the actors.  I felt like the people across the way were staring at me."

"Yes, yes," said Shoop, nodding, "but tell us about your observations during the performance."

"Everything seemed to be going along fine," Rocky replied.  "Of course, I had no way of knowing if there was anything that wasn't right as I'd never seen this production before."

"But you'd seen other productions?" asked Shoop.

"Not exactly," said Rocky. "I believe I've seen a film version of 'Importance of Being Earnest' several times. Can't quite remember the gist of the whole plot but most of it comes back to me. The friend who tries to woo the girl by changing his name to Earnest. A very famous drawing room comedy. Pamela's friend Joan was actually quite good as Lady Bracknell. Of course, we didn't see all that much of the show, Detective. The young woman who died collapsed in the middle of the first act."

"Can you describe what you remember about that event?" asked Shoop. "And the blackout immediately before?"

"Sure," said Rocky. "My main thought during the blackout was discomfort. I was close to the stage and I could hear people moving around on the stage doing things and it was pitch dark. Oh, they played music. I guess that was to cover the sounds of the set change, but you couldn't help but hear some of it. At least, we did because we were on the front row, practically on the stage."

"When the scene began between the actress who is your wife's friend and the one who collapsed?" prompted Shoop, waving his pencil at Rocky.

"Oh, yes," replied Rocky. "They were seated at this little table that was almost in front of us—maybe a few feet to our right. Joan had her back to us on the left side of the table, and the younger actress playing Gwendolyn was seated across from her, actually a few yards further down from us to our right. When she swallowed that liquid in that tea cup, Detective, I happened to be looking right at her face, and, believe me, I could tell that she had a definite unpleasant reaction to whatever she drank. Almost immediately, she started to choke and gasp. She clutched at her throat as if she was trying to either speak or maybe get the liquid from her throat. It all happened so fast. Her efforts were in vain and no one seemed to even realize the seriousness of her condition until she collapsed on the floor."

"Did she say anything?" asked Shoop.

"Not that I could make out," replied Rocky. "Certainly she was making sounds, but I wouldn't classify them as words."

"Mr. Barnes," said Shoop, flipping through the pages of his little book, apparently scanning over Rocky's testimony. "Is there anything else you saw or heard that night that you would like to add?"

"Not that I can think of," said Rocky.

"Doctor, um, Mrs. Barnes?" asked Shoop, turning and looking at Pamela who had remained quiet as she sat beside Rocky throughout his descriptions.

"That's pretty much the way I remember it too," she added. "I was seated on my husband's left. He was actually just a bit closer to the actress who died than I was. He had a better view of her face, I guess. Of course, I remember the look on her face as he describes it. It was just horrible. I was frozen when it happened. Truthfully, I didn't know anything about the play, as my husband does. I'd never seen it, so I thought it might be part of the plot when she fell on the floor, but then I glanced over at him and saw that he was aghast, so I assumed that the actress truly was in terrible distress. Everything he said I observed too, Shoop."

The detective looked up and then back and forth from husband to wife. Eventually, he closed his little book and extracted himself from the soft cushion of the arm chair.

"Dr. Barnes," he noted upon standing, "you seem to like furniture with soft cushions." Not waiting for a reply, he nodded at Officer Ryan who was still standing near the front door maintaining eye contact with Candide. Shoop shook hands with the couple and then exited in a swirl of overcoat, followed by the silent Ryan. With the intruders gone, Rocky turned to Pamela.

"Now I'm totally awake."

"Me too."

"Nothing like a midnight interrogation to get one's juices flowing," said Rocky with a lascivious smile.

"Rocky," she said. "Just what juices would those be?"

He grabbed her hand without a word and led her quietly to the bedroom. Candide who was still standing watch, pranced along behind.

## CHAPTER 14

The Friday night interrogation had not led to an eventful weekend, and Pamela had enjoyed her free days, returning to work Monday morning feeling refreshed.   Admittedly, Rocky had rejuvenated her spirits quite a bit after Shoop's departure and she felt ready to handle anything that the new week had in store.

Jane Marie was diligently at work in her little alcove when Pamela entered the main office.  Rays of sunlight wafted through the fall-colored trees outside of her window, painting the secretary's face with a warm glow.   The young woman looked up from her keyboard.

"Dr. Barnes!  Good morning!  A beautiful fall day, isn't it?"  Jane Marie was wearing a pumpkin-colored sweater over a deep chocolate brown dress that almost matched her shoulder-length curls.  She looked like a poster for autumn.

"Indeed, Jane Marie.   Hopefully this nice, calm weekend will herald an even calmer week ahead."

"From your mouth," said Jane Marie.   "My goodness, we don't need any more catastrophes!  My husband has been agonizing over this mess with the new theater and the Coffee Factory."

"Your husband?"

"He belongs to the Chamber of Commerce," she replied.   "Their entire downtown advisory board was counting on the relocation of the community theater to help boost the downtown area. You know, because it's in the Coffee Factory. Then, when that poor woman died...was murdered actually...in their opening production...well, it certainly doesn't help business. He says all the businesses in the downtown area are just horrified. They're demanding the police solve this murder immediately. Probably more because it's so bad for business, rather than because they care that much about the poor woman."

"Yes, their vested interest," noted Pamela.

"Of course, her father-in-law is in the Chamber too," replied Jane Marie. "I mean, the girl who died—Belinda Purvis. Tom Purvis of Purvis Autos. He's really pressing the police to solve this case, as you can well imagine."

"I don't have to imagine," responded Pamela, leaning against the secretary's desk. "Shoop was at my house on Friday night at midnight to interrogate Rocky."

"Midnight?"

"Yes," she said. "Oh, he claimed he thought we were both awake, but we weren't. He'd questioned me several days ago in my office, but he wanted to ask Rocky his version too because we had both been at the production and we were both seated fairly close to the young woman when she collapsed on stage."

"Oh, Dr. Barnes," said Jane Marie, shaking her head, "how horrible for you. To witness that and not be able to do anything."

"Truthfully, Jane Marie," she added, "as I told Shoop, I wasn't sure her collapse wasn't actually part of the show. You know, maybe the character was supposed to faint or something. It wasn't until the director came onto the stage and told the audience to leave that I was completely convinced that it wasn't planned."

"I can understand that," replied the secretary. "I would probably have felt the same way. I guess it's good that that detective did come out and question your husband—even if it was late—if it will help them track down whoever killed Belinda. I mean, the sooner they arrest the killer, the sooner the community theater can get the play up and running again."

"That's certainly what Joan wants," said Pamela, sitting on the edge of Jane Marie's desk.

"And the mayor!" added Jane Marie.

"James?" she asked.

"Yes," said the secretary. "My husband says he's been all over the police to speed up their investigation. He says it's a like a black eye on Reardon's face with this murder hanging over the city."

"If James Grant is involved," noted Pamela, tapping her finger on the top of Jane Marie's computer monitor, "things will move fast. He's a dynamo. Reardon was certainly lucky to get him for a mayor."

"Weren't we!" added Jane Marie. "Such an improvement over the former mayor! I don't think anything can sour my husband on local events now that James is directing things at city hall. But I know he's worried—and James is only one person. It's not like he can solve this murder all by himself. And my husband says downtown development is at a standstill until things get moving with the theater in the Coffee Factory and that's not going to happen until they solve this murder."

"They will," said Pamela emphatically, standing and gathering her belongings. "I have every faith in James, just as does your husband." She waved farewell to her friend and headed out of the main office of the Psychology Department and headed up to the second floor where her office was located.

Once inside, she unloaded her books and papers and placed her lunch bag and thermos in her small refrigerator. She never peeked inside her sack, wanting to keep each of Rocky's special meals an unexpected treat. He virtually never repeated himself, always providing her with nourishing and tasty sandwiches, salads, or various dishes that she could eat cold at her desk. He also sent her unusual beverages each day in her thermos, mostly fruit teas, but sometimes shakes or other unusual concoctions. Ooo, tea! She might never look at a cup—or thermos— —of tea in the same way again. Even so, she never tired of sitting down on her sofa each day and opening the surprise package that he made for her. The fact that Rocky loved to cook for her and their family never ceased to amaze her, as she perceived cooking as totally boring. But Rocky lavished love and attention on every meal he made and his interest in the culinary arts just seemed to grow with each passing year. Yes, she was a truly lucky wife.

Unpacked, she headed to her desk and picked up the telephone. She dialed a number she knew fairly well and James Grant, the town's new, young mayor answered almost immediately.

"James, it's Pamela Barnes."

"Calling my private line, Pamela. This must be serious."

"Just concern, James," she replied. "I was just talking with our departmental secretary who tells me that you're taking a personal interest in this recent murder that occurred during the community theater production."

"Yes, I am, Pamela," he said, "and I hear you were there the night it happened."

"I was."

"I would have been there myself but I had a last minute emergency," said James. Pamela could hear the regret in his voice. "Boy, I wish I'd been there. I never would have let that director release the audience before the police arrived. That was a huge mistake. Now, they have to track down audience members to question them and it's evidently proving almost impossible. There were over a hundred people there."

"I know," said Pamela. "You know Joan Bentley was in the production, James."

"Don't I know it," he replied. "I believe she contacted my secretary and personally extended an invitation to attend her opening night. Yes, that's right—*her* opening night. That's our Joan. Right, Pamela?"

"Yes, it is," agreed Pamela, chuckling. She and Joan had worked hard to help James in his recent bid for mayor—doing much more than just campaign chores. The two women had assisted the young man exonerate himself from an unfair murder charge. The three had remained friends ever since.

"So, you were there?" he asked her.

"Rocky and I were both in the front row," she replied sadly.

"I'm sure your acutely attuned scientific eyes—I should say, ears—would pick up any unexpected events that might assist the police."

"Better than that," she said. "I happened to make an audio recording for Arliss, who was unable to attend Joan's opening because her baby was sick. I gave it to Detective Shoop, who is head investigator on this case. I guess he's head investigator on every murder case in Reardon. I suspect there aren't any more detectives on the force."

James laughed. "Oh, there are more detectives," he said. "Shoop just happens to be the best. Believe me, we want—you want—the best investigator on this one, Pamela. Of course, we want to find the person who killed this poor young woman, but this murder impacts the entire community in a very adverse way."

"Our departmental secretary, Jane Marie Mira, was just saying that this morning."

"She's right," added James. "We have a lot of downtown businesses counting on this marriage between the community theater and the Coffee Factory to be a success. And if it's a success and brings in new customers, then all of the downtown businesses will benefit."

"I see," she said.

"Believe me, Pamela," he continued, "I know Belinda's family. I know her husband, her mother. I know her father-in-law, Tom Purvis, even better. He's a community leader. These are all fine people, but even more, these are all people who are working hard to make Reardon a better community—particularly the downtown."

"I can imagine her family—her husband—is devastated."

"Absolutely," he exclaimed. "Who would do such a thing? To put poison in this young woman's tea cup so she would not only die a horrible death, but to do it so she would die publicly?  It's almost like adding insult to injury.  As if the murderer wanted to see the woman die, which I'm assuming the person did."

"Did see her die?"

"Of course," he said.  "If the killer was backstage, he or she could peek through the curtains and watch the entire thing."

"I guess they could," said Pamela, remembering that the theater entrance she and Rocky had come through was indeed a curtained one.

"Do the police share any information with you?" she asked.  "Are they getting close to finding the killer? I mean, do they have any leads?"

"Shoop keeps things pretty close to his vest," replied James.  "I've asked him, but he just says he's hard at work."

"He does have my audio recording," she said forlornly.  "I'm afraid that won't do him much good though."

"Maybe it won't do him much good, Pamela," James said, "but I can imagine it might do you some good.  I assume you made a copy of the recording?"

"Now how did you know that?"

"I can't imagine you wouldn't," he said, laughing. "Pamela Barnes, acoustic crime fighter.  I can't imagine you'd let go of an audio recording of a crime without first making a copy for yourself."

"Okay, so I did," she said.

"So, use it," he directed her.  "There must be something on that recording that would provide a hint about this murder.  If anyone can extract that something, Pamela, it would be you.  I know from experience."

"Believe me, James," she told him, "I've been doing just that."

"Keep at it, Pamela," he said encouraging. "I'll do my part to help track down this murderer. You do your part. And your part is to analyze that recording and try to find something on it that will help the police catch the killer."

"I'll do my best," she assured him. They discussed other more pleasant topics and eventually Pamela said goodbye and hung up. Then she just sat there with the receiver in her hands, gnawing on her lower lip as she contemplated James's admonition.

## CHAPTER 15

Pamela's morning classes went by smoothly. Her lectures seemed to be understood and she apparently was able to answer her students' questions with appropriate responses. As they weren't all that far into the semester, most students were not yet that worried about final projects and exams. Most would wait until the last minute to become concerned, so the months between the start of classes in the fall and the end of the first semester in December were typically blissfully free of trauma.

She wandered back to her office from the second floor lecture hall following her early afternoon intro class, sipping from her thermos. She pulled her key chain from the depths of her big handbag and opened her office door. She could tell as she glanced down the corridor that neither Joan nor Willard were in their offices. She knew that they both had classes at this hour too but in more distant locations so they would probably not arrive back for some minutes. Willard, of course, would arrive latest as his ambulatory problems made walking extremely difficult. She had often suggested that he request his classes be held in more nearby classrooms, which could certainly be arranged given Willard's medical needs, but the professor was adamant that he receive no special treatment because of his ailments.

The sounds from the campus outside her window beckoned her and she wandered over to her window and glanced down at the activity below. Many students strode purposefully back and forth on the campus pathways. From her window she could see sidewalks that led to five or six different campus buildings, including the Student Union, the largest of them, which was visible on the opposite side of a swampy lake placed strategically in the center of the grassy area. Several wrought iron benches lined the lake and a few students were seated there, some eating lunch and some studying.

As she turned and placed her belongings on her desk, still clutching her thermos, Joan appeared in her doorway. Pamela took a sip of her orange-mango tea.

"Lord," declared Joan, flopping uninvited into her chair by the door, "what a morning! It's far too early for them to be this paranoid!" She clutched her key chain but let her body droop, her arms hanging limp at her sides.

"Paranoid?" asked Pamela, still standing behind her desk, her lips savoring the delicious tea from the thermos. She just couldn't give up Rocky's specialty tea drinks because of what had happened at the theater.

"You know how they are," said Joan, pulling herself upright. "They want to know every question on the final exam! As if I've even made up the final exam yet. Foolish students. They think I plan that far ahead. Of course, I let them think that I do!" She gave Pamela an impish smile.

"You would," said Pamela, wandering over to her couch and sinking into its soft cushions. She leaned back against the armrest and toasted Joan with her thermos. "Cheers to you!"

"Yes," said Joan. "Cheers to me!  Keep the little buggers on their best behavior."

"Any news about the play?" asked Pamela.

"You mean any news about the police investigation or any news about when it will be restaged?"

"Either."

"Ron did call me yesterday," Joan said succinctly, crossing one leg and placing her hands neatly on top. The movement made her gold charm bracelet tinkle. "He's found a new Gwendolyn."

"That's good," said Pamela.  "Do you know who it is?"

"I don't know her personally," said Joan, "but Ron has evidently worked with her before and claims that she'll be wonderful."

"So why wasn't she in the performance to begin with?"

"Oh, I don't know," said Joan, waving her hand, the bracelet glittering in the sunshine that fluttered in through Pamela's window.  "I think he said she hadn't auditioned because of some sort of conflict, but evidently, that was resolved and she was happy to have the part."

"I can imagine," answered Pamela.  "I mean, she didn't even have to try out.  Like you did."

"I know," agreed Joan.  "It does seem unfair, but I'm just glad we have a new Gwendolyn and we can start rehearsals again."

"You have to start all over?" asked Pamela, dropping her low heels and pulling her feet up onto her sofa.

"Of course, Pamela," said Joan.  "This new woman doesn't know the play at all.  She'll have to be worked into it."

"Couldn't the director just do that," suggested Pamela, "so the rest of the cast doesn't have to go through it all over again?"

"Oh, Good Lord," cried Joan, arms in the air, "you simply don't understand the theater, my dear!"

Arliss popped suddenly into the office doorway.

"What doesn't she understand?" asked the young lab director, as she slipped between her two friends and pulled out Pamela's desk chair and straddled it, giving it a shove backwards with her feet on the desk.

"The theater," said Joan.  "We have a new Gwendolyn!"

"That's good," said Arliss, from her new spot.  "This smells good, Pam."  She pointed at the brown paper sack on the desk which contained the remains of Pamela's lunch.

"Cranberry orange bread with an olive filling," said Pamela as she described the contents of the bag.

"Didn't you eat it all?" asked Arliss, opening the bag and peering inside.

"Rocky gives me far too much food," she whined.

"Oooo!" cried Arliss, taking a deep breath from the interior of the bag.  "Can I have a bite?"

"Help yourself," said Pamela, as Arliss grabbed a wax paper-wrapped sandwich and scarfed it down.

"I haven't had a decent meal in ages," she said, pushing the fly-away locks out of her face with the back of her hand as she savored the remnants of Pamela's lunch.  "All it's been lately is Noah, Noah, Noah!"

"He's still sick?" asked Pamela.

"No," replied Arliss, her mouth full, "he's better, but still demanding and cranky. He's keeping us up late at night. I guess maybe we got into a habit of attending to his every cry and now he likes that."

"I smell a spoiled baby," said Joan, pulling down her glasses and peering at Arliss over the top.

"He's not spoiled, Joan," replied Arliss, slapping down her feet from the desk top to the floor.

"Ladies!" cried Pamela, sitting up on the sofa, bare feet on the cold floor. "Let's not argue! As I see it, it's good news all around. Joan's play is soon up and running again. Arliss's baby is better. Things are looking up all around."

"Except for that poor woman who was murdered," said Arliss with a shrug. "They're not looking up for her."

"No," agreed Pamela, "but hopefully, the police will get to the bottom of that soon. Hopefully, they'll find the killer and put all this to rest."

"Yes, the sooner, the better," said Joan. "Having the murder unsolved just puts a terrible pall over our production."

"That's one reason," agreed Pamela with a shrug, "but I'm guessing her family is more concerned about justice for their daughter—and wife."

"Of course," said Joan. "That goes without saying."

"Does it, Joan?" asked Arliss.

"Anyway," said Pamela, jumping into the conversation again, as it appeared that her two friends might come to blows over this issue. "Anyway, I've been discussing things with Shoop, and as you both know, I've got that audio recording of the...murder. I even talked with James this morning!"

"How is James?" asked Joan.

"Concerned," said Pamela, "as you both are. He's of course concerned that the killer be caught, as you note, Arliss. However, he's also concerned as Joan is that the show be restaged because he believes it will be a boon to business in the downtown area."

"Of course it will," said Joan, beaming beatifically. "That's just what I was saying."

"He said the downtown businesses were really counting on the theater's new location helping improve business at the Coffee Factory—and by extension, the entire downtown area," explained Pamela.

"You see!" added Joan with a smile at Arliss.

"It got me thinking," said Pamela as she stared at the books in the tall shelf on the opposite side of her office.

"What?" asked Arliss, leaning her elbows on the desk as she continued to nibble on Pamela's leftover sandwich. "What are you thinking?"

"Yes, Pamela," added Joan, attempting to break Pamela's reverie. "Just what are you thinking?"

"I'm thinking that we should do our part to help the downtown area," said Pamela.

"You mean we should go shopping in downtown Reardon?" asked Arliss. "Buy clothes? What? I guess Noah could use some more onesies."

"I'm never averse to a girls' shopping trip," added Joan, swinging her key ring.

"We could do that," said Pamela, sitting up straight on the edge of her sofa. "I was really just thinking about the Coffee Factory. If the two of you don't have anything planned for this afternoon, would you be opposed to a visit for an early supper? Or maybe just a late-afternoon snack?"

"Not me!" said Arliss.  "This sandwich of yours was great, Pam!  But it just made me hungry.  The Coffee Factory has some great desserts."

"They do," said Joan.  "I should be revising that article for *Experimental Psychological Research Design* that I'm supposed to get done by next week, but a yummy dessert could divert me from my agenda."

"And, maybe," suggested Pamela, "we can finagle a look at the theater?"

"Why would we need to finagle a look?" asked Joan. "I spent hours of time rehearsing upstairs of the Coffee Factory, and probably have that much time logged downstairs eating and drinking in the Factory.  Those waitresses know me like a sister.  There's no reason why they wouldn't let me up there to look around."

"But, Joan," said Pamela, "that was before it became a crime scene."

"Yes," agreed Arliss, "there may be yellow police tape all over the place now, Joan."

"Whether there is or isn't," cried Joan, "they will surely let cast members up there.  I mean, we might have left important belongings off-stage."

"Did you?" asked Pamela.

"No," said Joan, deflated.  "But I can pretend that I did.  After all, I am an actress."

"Can you wait a minute while I check with my sitter?" asked Arliss.  She pulled a cell phone from the back pocket of her trousers and tapped in a few numbers.  "Hey, Mia!  It's Arliss.  How's Noah?" She listened as the voice at the other end apparently began to describe some humorous behavior of baby Noah. Arliss continued to nod as she sat back down and relaxed with her feet back up on the desk.

"At this rate," whispered Joan to Pamela, "we won't even make it there for dinner."

"Shhh!" said Pamela, continuing to listen to the one-sided telephone conversation between Arliss and her babysitter. "No office hours today?" she asked Joan.

"This morning," said Joan. "You?"

"Same."

"Oh, no!" screeched Arliss into the phone. Joan and Pamela froze and turned to Arliss whose face was white. "He didn't!" She continued to listen, her nods obviously unseen by the babysitter. Eventually, the phone call ended and Arliss closed her cell phone and looked up into the panic-stricken faces of her friends.

"What's wrong?" asked Pamela.

"He crawled!" announced Arliss.

"Oh, is that all!" said Joan with a sigh of relief. "It sounded from your reaction that he was in anaphylactic shock!"

"No!" cried Arliss. "Mia said she had him on the carpet and his little red truck was over by the chair, and he couldn't get it, so he just pushed himself up on his knees and crawled right over to it! Isn't he amazing!" Tears appeared at the corner of her eyes.

"Truly amazing!" said Joan. "I'm sure no other baby in the entire world could accomplish such a feat!"

"Joan," chided Pamela. "It's wonderful, Arliss. Sorry you weren't there for it. But you'll see it soon. So? Ladies? Are we still going to the Coffee Factory?"

"Oh, why not!" said Arliss, wiping her eyes with the sleeve of her bulky sweater. "We can celebrate Noah crawling!"

"Yes, let's!" smirked Joan.

"To the Coffee Factory!" called out Pamela as the three professors headed out of Blake Hall.

## CHAPTER 16

"Dr. Bentley!" exclaimed a waitress as the three women entered the deserted Coffee Factory. The outside window of the establishment still proclaimed the upcoming opening night with a full display, complete with colorful banner and photographs of all the cast members. Joan's picture was placed prominently in the center at the top.

"Hello, Emily," responded Joan. "My colleagues and I decided to drop by for an early supper." She motioned to Pamela and Arliss, now depositing their purses and jackets on the spiked backs of the captains' chairs that surrounded the square table in the center of the deserted restaurant.

"Oh, Dr. Barnes!" exclaimed the young waitress, waving her order pad and pencil at Pamela. "I had you for Intro to Psych last year. You probably don't remember me; there were hundreds of students…"

"I believe I do, Emily," said Pamela, looking up from the large menu that Emily had distributed to the three women. "I always remember good students." She smiled at the waitress who blushed and focused her attention on her order pad.

"The Factory is empty," noted Joan, looking around. "I hope this isn't normal for you, Emily."

"I'm afraid so, Dr. Bentley," replied the young woman. "Ever since…you know. Ever since opening night."

"Yes," said Joan, "such a disaster!"  She clucked and shook her head sadly.  Then, she abruptly seemed to change gears.  "But, Emily, I hope you heard that we will be restaging the play.  Ron found a new Gwendolyn.  Isn't that wonderful?"

"Oh, Dr. Bentley!" exclaimed Emily, clutching her booklet to her chest. "That's fabulous!  Everyone has just been miserable since that night.  Such a terrible tragedy.  And it's been just awful for business.  Mr. Barge has been at his wits' end.  All of us are scared we'll be fired at any minute.  I'm just thrilled you came in.  Oh, my!  You must think I'm a loon.  What can I get you, ladies?"  She held out her order book and turned to Pamela who was intently perusing the lengthy menu.

"Oh, my!  It's been a long time since I've been here," she said.  "You've really expanded your menu."

"Yes," replied Emily.  "This was all in anticipation of an increase in business when the little theater starting drawing customers in."

"What are you going to have, Arliss?" Pamela asked, looking sideways at Arliss who was virtually buried in the giant menu.

"I'm starving," said Arliss.  "I think a burger and fries.  How about this Factory Flipper?"

"It's delicious!" said Emily. "And it's huge.  So if you're really hungry, it's a good choice."

"That sounds good to me too," added Pamela, placing her menu on the table.

"I'll have the chicken salad with lemon muffins," announced Joan.  "I know that's good.  I've had it before.  The cast would eat here a lot while we were rehearsing.  Their muffins are to die for.  I mean, they're delicious." She tipped her head down and scowled at her faux pas.

"And beverages?" asked the waitress, undeterred.

"What's the special?" asked Joan, sitting up sprightly.

"Pomegranate coffee," said the waitress. "It's yummy!" She gave a little shake of her shoulders and a broad smile.

"Sounds good to me!" chimed in Pamela, handing her menu to Emily.

"Me too!" said Arliss, adding hers to the pile.

"Make that three!" finished Joan, placing her menu on top of the other two. The young waitress gathered the large menus that were starting to slip from her arms.

"Be right back with your coffees," she said and turned and disappeared into a curtained opening under the staircase that ran up the side of the interior wall, leading to the second floor where the theater held its performances.

"It's convenient to have the theater upstairs, isn't it, Joan?" asked Pamela. "I guess you and the other actors spent a lot of time down here."

"We did," she replied. "After late night rehearsals, we were all usually so keyed up that we just couldn't go home, so we'd gather here and bond."

"You must have gotten to know the people in the cast really well," added Arliss.

"I did—some of them, at least," replied Joan. "I'd never been in a theatrical production before, but you work together so closely and so long that you do begin to feel like a family. I feel a little lost not being able to see them on a regular basis like we used to do." She sighed. Emily arrived with the three coffees. The aroma from the mugs wafted around the table and the women immediately began to sip their drinks.

"Heavenly," said Pamela.   She knew she wasn't drinking real coffee as the Coffee Factory was well known for their alternative coffee beverages.   The original owner, Romulus Reardon, who had founded the factory during the Civil War to produce artificial coffee for the Confederacy when Union blockades prevented supplies of regular coffee beans from getting through, was their town's namesake.  Over the years, the Reardon Coffee Factory had become known for its alternative coffees created from various plants that were grown in the area—and now some that were not even indigenous to the locale.  It was actually one of Reardon's few tourist attractions and even the locals enjoyed dining at the Coffee Factory which was housed in the actual building where Romulus Reardon had first created his world-famous beverages.

"Yum," agreed Arliss.   Joan was apparently speechless as she sipped quietly on her drink.

"Emily," said Pamela, looking around and determining that the waitress was not at all busy.  "I'm curious.  What's your schedule like?"

"You mean my work schedule here, Dr. Barnes?" asked the waitress.  "I'm part time. I only work the night shift, from five to midnight when we close.  I don't work every day because I'm still in school. Mr. Barge is really nice about working our schedules around our classes."

"Have they had to lay off anyone since the...since the production closed?" she asked.  Joan gave her a quick, evil glance.

"So far, no, but they have cut back our hours," she replied.  "As you can tell, we're not really very busy."

She looked around the empty restaurant. "Usually we'd be at least half full at this time. I guess people are frightened."

"Why?" asked Joan.

"I don't know," said Emily. "They certainly don't think Belinda—I mean, Mrs. Purvis—was poisoned by our food, I hope."

"No," said Pamela, "the police have made it clear that Belinda died during the production from drinking tea that was laced with poison. It was in her cup onstage. There's been no suggestion that she was poisoned by food from the Factory."

"I know," agreed Joan. "People make the strangest connections. There's no reason for anyone to be frightened of the Coffee Factory or afraid to eat the food here."

"You'd think," suggested Arliss, still slurping the warm pomegranate coffee drink in her mug, "you'd have more customers. Most people are usually such looky-loos when it comes to murders. You'd think they'd all be down here wanting to see where this poor girl met her untimely end."

"Yuck, Arliss," said Pamela, "how gruesome. I don't really think people do that. Do you?"

"Of course they do," said Arliss, wiping her hair from her face. "Haven't you ever seen the line of traffic that forms after a car crash? People are drawn to tragedies."

"Not if they think they might be in danger," said Joan, holding her coffee in the air, the aroma wafting around as she waved it like a pointer. "Arliss may be right. People might connect the Factory with the theater upstairs and connect a poisoning in one location with a possible poisoning in the other. That might very well account for the decrease in business here."

At that moment, a large man wearing dark trousers, a glistening white dress shirt, and a dark green apron, entered from between the curtains under the staircase. He was a handsome man for as round as he was, with a head full of curly brown hair and a beard and mustache that matched exactly. His eyes twinkled and a gold earring in his right earlobe sparkled only dully in comparison. He came to the table.

"Missy Joan," he said, grabbing her hand, bending low and placing a kiss on the back of Joan's hand. "It is a pleasure and an honor to have you once again in my establishment."

"Silvus!" replied Joan, smiling sweetly, maybe even flirtatiously at the man, and then turned to her friends. "I'd like you to meet my friends, Dr. Barnes and Mrs. Goodman, colleagues from the Psychology Department. Pam, Arliss, this is Silvus Barge, the owner of the Coffee Factory."

"Delighted to meet you, ladies," he swooned as he moved elegantly to each and placed swift kisses on their hands as well. "Surely, you are not the famous Pamela Barnes? The one who solves all the murders?"

"I doubt I'm that famous," said Pamela softly in an attempt to discourage his raving. Barge was waving his arms around as he mentioned her name. Luckily they were the only people in the restaurant.

"What a treat to have you back at the Factory, Missy Joan," continued Barge, now focused on Joan, much to Pamela's relief. "I so miss you and the cast of the play enlivening this place until the wee hours of the morning. Fabulous!" His small eyes were like little sapphires peeking out of the soft velvet folds of an elegant jewelry box.

"I'm so sad to see the Factory empty like this, Silvus," said Joan forlornly as she looked around the deserted place.

"Oh, my dear Missy Joan," he said, inhaling deeply and thoughtfully. "I have faith!  You must have faith! That director of yours, that Ron Whitcomb, he is a dynamo, is he not?  He will surely get the theatrical ball rolling again and our little eatery will come alive once more!"  He rubbed his large, stubby hands on the bottom of his green apron.

"I certainly hope so," said Joan.  "Did you hear that they've recast Belinda's role?"

"Wonderful!" exclaimed the owner.  "So sad for Miss Belinda!  Such a lovely young lady, but, life it goes on, you know.  Many people here in Reardon, especially in the downtown, we are counting on the theater."

"How is the theater, Silvus?" asked Joan.

"You mean, upstairs?  The little stage?" he asked, somewhat confused.  "It is just as it was the night of... the night of the show, you know.  I would not touch anything.  Of course, the police, they tell me to not touch anything, and I, of course, would not touch anything anyway."

"Silvus," said Joan, "would it be okay if I showed the theater to my friends?  While we wait for our dinners?"

"Why, of course!" he cried.  "Let me escort you, ladies!"  He motioned for the women to follow him, which they did.  Pamela was actually delighted to take another look at the crime scene in the cold light of day, without all the attendant excitement.

"Come on, Arliss," said Joan, pulling on her friend's sleeve. "You can see where I had my almost-debut!"

"What about my sandwich?" cried Arliss, pointing at the kitchen and the coffee mugs still sitting half-full on the table.

"Oh, we'll be right back," said Joan, gesturing for them to follow her. Silvus was heading towards the staircase that led to the second floor. "Just leave your things at your seat. No one will bother them."

"Missy Joan, she is right," called out Silvus Barge, turning back, "there is no one to bother your belongings. Come, ladies! I will show you around the Reardon Little Theater's new home!"

Arliss reluctantly crawled out of her seat with one last quick slurp of her pomegranate coffee and a longing look at the kitchen. She evidently hoped that her sandwich would arrive and prevent her from traipsing upstairs to look at an empty theater, which she was doing just for Joan's benefit.

The little caravan headed up the steep, narrow wooden steps. They creaked with each footstep just as they had the night of the production, Pamela recalled. When they reached the top, Silvus Barge pulled back a maroon velvet curtain and the three women entered into the now empty Reardon Community Theater.

## CHAPTER 17

"Are we allowed in here?" Pamela asked the large restaurateur who was puffing noticeably from the long climb.

"Oh, indeed!" he said with a labored smile. "The police actually just finished collecting all of their evidence this morning. They removed the yellow tape and told us we were free to use the second floor again."

"I'm sure Ron will be thrilled!" cried Joan. "Now that he has a new Gwendolyn, we can start rehearsals again."

Barge gestured for the women to enter.

"I've learned quite a bit about our new little theater since the group has taken up residence above the Factory," he said proudly. "Ron has educated me. This method of staging is called 'theater-in-the-round' because the audience sits on all sides. Our little stage, she is a true 'theater-in-the-round' unlike some with the same name that seat audience members only on three sides. The acting takes place in the center on this ground level—you see—and the audience is seated on all sides in progressively higher and higher rows. This is different from proscenium staging which is the more traditional where the audience is seated only on one side and the play takes place on a stage— sometimes even a raised stage which occurs when the audience area is not raised as ours is."

"Why didn't the theater decide to create a proscenium stage?" asked Pamela.

"I am not totally sure," replied Barge, "but I understand from hearing some of the theater people talking that this 'in-the-round' method is cheaper."

"I believe it is," said Joan, "although there may be other reasons. I'm not all that involved with the local theater. This is my first production, but I've heard some of them discuss it and also you can see that the staging is quite simple. It has to be because if you had a lot of fancy scenery the audience wouldn't be able to see all of the action—and it would be much too hard to change sets between acts."

"I can see that," said Pamela. "Actually, I wasn't bothered by it. At first, I thought I might miss having all the elaborate sets that you expect when you see a play on a regular stage, but once I got into the play, I enjoyed being so close to the action, that I totally forgot about the sparse furnishings."

"I think that's what they're counting on," noted Barge. "They don't have a huge budget. And who knows what effect—I mean monetary effect—this murder will have on attendance. It might dampen it, but then again, it might bring out a lot of people looking for a cheap thrill."

"Won't it freak you out to be up here where that woman died, Joan?" asked Arliss, hesitating a bit behind the group.

The women entered the semi-darkened theater, Joan taking the lead. She pulled them through the four-tiered bleacher entrance to the edge of the stage. Without the bright stage lights and audience filling all the seats, the little theater seemed a bit woebegone, thought Pamela. She noticed that the stage furniture remained just as it had been when Belinda Purvis had collapsed. One overhead Klieg light was all the illumination available and the entire space seemed forlorn and dingy. Silvus Barge remained at the edge of the stage, leaning against one of the audience chairs, apparently getting his breath.

"Of course not!" replied Joan in response to Arliss's question. "I trust the local police to get to the bottom of this. I'm sure it doesn't involve any of the cast. I know them all and I can't believe any of them would do such a thing. They were all excited about opening night—just as I was." She wandered around the stage, looking, Pamela thought, as comfortable as she had as Lady Bracknell during the performance.

"Is that where the actress was sitting?" asked Arliss, edging onto the stage area with Pamela and Joan, and pointing at the small table by the edge.

"Yes," replied Joan. She swooped over to the table and seated herself in the position she had been in when the fatal event had occurred. "I was here." She gestured dramatically and Arliss scooted over and sat in a seat on the opposite side of the stage where she could see Joan's face.

"I was here," added Pamela, moving to the audience seat in the front row on the opposite side, several feet behind Joan. "At least, I think this is the seat I was in." She looked around at the seats next to her on both sides. "It's hard to tell without all of the other audience members here."

"You can just check your ticket stub if you still have it," called out Silvus Barge, who had seated himself by the main entrance. "All of the seats are reserved. Just look at the arm of your seat. You'll see its number."

Pamela looked down as directed and noticed that the arm of her seat did indicate a letter and number. It was "C6." The seat to her right was "C7." That had been Rocky's seat.

"The theater is divided into quadrants—A, B, C, and D. The letter indicates the quadrant and the number indicates the particular seat. They start numbering the seats from the left end of the first row of each quadrant, then continue with the left end of the second row, and so on. There are ten seats in each row and four rows in each quadrant, so 160 seats in the house. That's the most important part of the theater for the Factory because we have to train the wait staff to know the seating arrangement as they sell a lot of tickets to patrons downstairs," he explained, obviously proud of the knowledge he had acquired about his new business venture.

Joan was now touching the small table.

"Where are the props, Silvus?" she asked.

"Oh, the police took everything from that table, Miss Joan," he said. "The cup that Miss Belinda drank from, obviously, because it contained poison. But they took your cup too and the tea pot."

"Did they take any of our other props?" she asked, rising and heading towards the curtained entrance across from the main entrance where they had come in.

"No," he replied. "I don't think so. I've only been up here a few times, and that was when the police were here, sort of showing them around backstage. I think everything backstage is as it was on opening night."

"Good," announced Joan. "Pamela, Arliss, come!" She gestured to her friends to follow her as she swooped through the heavy curtains across the way from the entrance. Pamela gave a shrug to Arliss who was still seated across the stage from her and the two friends rose and followed Joan backstage. Silvus Barge attempted to extract his large frame from the small seat in which he was seated, but eventually gave up and remained where he was, content to let the women examine the backstage area alone.

"We'll be back, Silvus!" Joan called as she left, which evidently was sufficient reason for Silvus to remain in his seat.

As the friends entered the backstage area, the lighting became even bleaker and more subdued than in the main stage area. Pamela could see long tables set against dingy walls and several doors slightly opened that apparently led into small rooms or closets. There were hanging pipes and dangling light bulbs placed strategically. What appeared to be a lectern stood near the entrance. On it, Pamela could see a walkie-talkie, a clipboard, and a metal tray that held several small items such as a pipe and some handkerchiefs.

"This is the stage manager's post," said Joan, pointing to the lectern. "John—our stage manager— runs the show backstage. He also runs the light cues." She pointed to a board on the wall behind the lectern where several rows of switches had apparently been jerry-rigged and color-coded. All the handles were in the down position. "Those control all the stage lights."

Joan led Pamela and Arliss further back into the darkened backstage, pointing at various things as she went.

"Our prop table," she said, indicating a long table against a wall. "John sets the props on this table each night. You can see he has the props divided by scene. On the left are the Act One props. Then, here in the center are the Act Two props. We know where to pick up each hand prop we use and we're supposed to return it to its proper place."

"And is this where the teapot and tea cups were kept?" asked Pamela.

"Yes," said Joan. She gestured around the area. "And, Pamela, as you can see, the props are all left out where anyone might touch them, or add something..."

"Such as poison," noted Arliss.

"Yes," agreed Joan.

"But only the cast and crew could do that, couldn't they, Joan?" asked Pamela, looking around for other entrances.

"Come here," said Joan, leading them further back around the far side of the stage itself which was completely surrounded with the maroon velvet. She led them to a push-out external door that she opened for them and leaned out. "An outside exit. We could enter the theater this way or through the restaurant if it was before the audience was let in. Most of us came in this way."

Pamela peeked out the door. A long, wobbly-looking set of stairs led down two flights to the ground below behind the Coffee Factory. A grassy parking lot behind the building revealed several cars, probably belonging to Silvus Barge and Factory workers.

"Can anyone park there?" asked Arliss.

"Yes," replied Joan, "of course, mostly just people who work at the Factory do, and actors during rehearsals."

"What about audience members for the shows?" asked Arliss.

"No," said Joan, "they're encouraged to use the public parking across the street. This lot is private for the Factory and most customers don't know about it."

"Most," said Pamela. "But surely, some do. You have to admit, Joan, that it would be extremely easy for some stranger to park there, slip up here by these steps, slip backstage during a scene, and drop poison in that cup."

"Maybe," said Joan, "but that would assume that that person would never be noticed by anyone backstage and that's unlikely. John was always backstage. I can't believe he wouldn't notice a stranger messing about with the props on the prop table."

"There must have been times when he was totally busy with light cues," said Pamela.

"Or during a blackout," added Arliss.

"I suppose it's possible," agreed Joan. She led them further back to a long metal rack holding a dozen or so period costumes.

"These are my outfits," she announced, as she pointed to several of the fancier dresses. "Aren't they fabulous?"

"They are," said Arliss. "Now, can we get out of here and go eat our sandwiches? I'm starving."

"Humph!" cried Joan. "I thought you might like a tour."

"It's quite interesting, Joan," said Pamela, attempting to mediate what appeared to be an approaching argument between her friends. Joan, however, flounced her way back through the curtain entrance and onto the stage where Silvus appeared to have drifted off in the seat by the far entrance. He was snoring loudly.

"Silvus!" called out Joan as the women returned. "We're back!" The man shook himself and his tiny eyes popped open.

"Ooo! Lordy, lordy!" he exclaimed. "I drifted off there. These seats are much too comfortable."

The three friends laughed and moved back into the main stage area. Now, possibly emboldened by their visit backstage, they all sauntered around, glancing up at the seats.

"Did you find anything you were looking for back there, ladies?" he asked.

"I was just showing them around, Silvus," said Joan.

"No clues, Dr. Barnes?" he asked Pamela.

"Oh, I'll leave that up to the police," she said smiling.

"That's not what I've heard," he responded, tugging his body from the chair and meeting the women in the center of the stage.

"I guess we can go," said Joan a bit sadly. "Since Pamela hasn't found any clues."

"It doesn't appear likely, at least from what Joan says, that the killer would have entered from outside," said Pamela. "So, it does look like it has to be someone in the cast or crew."

"Or the audience," added Arliss.

The little foursome trudged down the rickety staircase and back to the restaurant below, where much to Arliss's joy, plates of sandwiches awaited them.

## CHAPTER 18

Much later that night, Pamela and Rocky were snuggled in bed, Candide resigned to his spot under the bed. Pamela had told her husband about her spur-of-the-moment outing with her friends to the Coffee Factory for an early dinner and their tour of the theater upstairs conducted by the Factory's owner and, of course, Joan.

"It looked, I don't know, sad," she said softly, cuddled up in his arms in the dark.

"What looked sad?"

"The theater. Maybe because there weren't any of those bright colorful stage lights, or the fancy period costumes."

"Or the actors!" he added.

"I guess," she said. "It all seemed so dreary and quiet."

"I'm sure part of it is because you know that woman died there," he suggested, squeezing her warmly.

"I suppose." She shook her head and he could feel it even if he couldn't see it.

"What?" he grumbled.

"It seemed smaller too."

"Smaller?"

"You know, the whole place. It's really quite small."

"I thought it held hundreds of people," he argued, pulling away a bit on an elbow.

"It does; it holds 160.  The restaurant owner, Silvus Barge, says each quadrant seats forty."

"That's a lot," he said.  "For a community theater.  If I remember correctly, the whole place was full."

"It was.  Opening night was a full house. Joan took us backstage too," she added.  "She showed us where they keep the props and the costumes.  They have some fellow who stays at a desk by that far entrance and coordinates everything.  He runs the lights from there too."

"Does he set all the props?"

"No, the actors set the props themselves.  Joan said they rehearsed the set changes as part of the show. The director, Ron Whitcomb, would actually time the set changes.  Joan had a specific job.  I think she said placing a suitcase by an entrance.  I'm not sure."

"Who set the tea cups?" he asked.

"Just what the police wanted to know, but unfortunately, Belinda set the tea service herself during that scene.  Of course, before she brought those props on stage, they were just sitting on a table backstage.   Joan showed us.   Anyone could have tampered with them.   There's also a door to the outside backstage that leads to a parking lot behind the Factory.  It's possible that someone could have slipped in during the production and put the poison in the cup while most of the actors were on stage and the stage manager was busy focused on the show."

Rocky pulled his arm up and leaned back against their headboard.  Pamela continued her description, grateful that her husband was willing to listen to her late night musings.

"Joan is convinced that it wasn't anyone in the cast," she said.  "I have no idea what the police think."

"No one saw anyone enter from outside, did they?" he asked.  Candide scooted out from under the bed when he heard the couple talking.  Conversation often led to eating.

"Have you listened to that recording you made?" he asked her, crossing his arms and peering over at her. "You're evidently keen on getting involved in this case it seems."

"Rocky, how can I help but be keen, as you say?  My best friend is possibly a suspect.  I have a potential clue with knowledge that might bear on understanding its content.  Plus, the whole awful episode just is a blight on the eye of the town, particularly the downtown. James is concerned, really concerned.  And you know how much I admire him.  Joan too."

She knew Rocky admired the young mayor as much as she did.  Any Reardon resident who had suffered through the administration of the previous mayor could not help but be encouraged by the present occupant's honesty and enthusiasm for improving their little community.

"You won't get any arguments from me, Babe," he said.  "I won't stop you from listening and analyzing that show recording all you want.  I can't imagine what you'd hear on it that would help you figure out who put that poison in the tea cup, but if you do, fantastic!"

"You know, Rocky," she said, a finger on his cheek, "you can help the efforts to track down the person who poisoned Belinda Purvis."

"Me?" he cried.  "I doubt it."

"You were there," she said, reminding him.  "You were actually seated closer to the...action, so to speak, than even I was.  You saw the victim's face as she drank the poison.  You saw the cup on the table.  You saw her reaction when she drank.  You're an observant fellow.  Maybe you remember something that I don't."

"As I said to your buddy Shoop the other night, I doubt it.  Truthfully, I wasn't much of an enthusiastic audience member, if you recall.  I felt uncomfortable.  On the spot.  Of course, I didn't wish any harm to any of the performers but when the show was cancelled, I'll have to admit, I wasn't disappointed.  I was rather glad to be out of there."

"That could be beneficial, actually.  I was paying close attention because I was enjoying myself and was all involved in the story.  I guess at first when the actress responded the way she did, I thought it was just part of the play and I really didn't think that much of it.  It wasn't until the director interrupted the production that I began to realize that she wasn't just acting.  You may have realized that sooner and maybe noticed something that I didn't."

"I may have realized it sooner, I guess," he said, "because I am somewhat familiar with the play, and I know that no one dies on stage."

"There!" she said, pointing her finger at his nose.  "So your observational juices were flowing, so to speak."

"Hmm," he sneered.

"So?" she insisted.  "Do you remember anything unusual?"

"Other than the fact that an actress died a horrible death during the middle of a play?"

"Other than that."

"Not really," he said, deflated.  "Sorry I can't help you.  What else would we be looking for?  The audience didn't see the killer put the poison in the cup."

"No," she said immediately, "because it would have had to have been put in backstage."

"And it would have had to have been someone who knew which cup to add it to," he said.

"Right," she said. "Joan made it clear how the killer probably knew that. Her cup had the lemon slice and Belinda's didn't."

"But wouldn't only cast members know that?" he asked. "You said Joan doesn't suspect cast members."

"True," replied Pamela. "If someone just wandered in from outside and dropped poison in Belinda's cup, how would they know that Belinda would be the one to drink from that particular cup?"

"Unless they knew the play," he said, "or had been watching rehearsals, or knew someone in the play who had told them about the way the tea cups were differentiated."

"And who would know that?" she asked. "I suppose Shoop has asked all the actors what they've told other people about the play. According to Joan, the only people other than cast members involved in the production are Ron Whitcomb, the director, the stage manager John, and a costume manager."

"Surely Shoop has questioned all of them," he noted.

"Surely," she agreed, nodding quizzically. "You said watching rehearsals."

"Yes."

"Silvus Barge said that the waitresses and staff of the Coffee Factory often peeked in on rehearsals. They all had to understand the seating arrangement of the theater so that if someone came into the Coffee Factory and wanted to buy a ticket, they could sell it to them—and explain to them about the theater. I guess potential patrons could even go upstairs and look at the theater and select their own seats."

"That sounds like something Shoop needs to check out," he said.

"If he hasn't already," she replied.  "I know he's tried to track down all the audience members who were there the night of the murder.  They were easily able to find those who were season ticket holders, but people who just came at the door or who bought single tickets are harder to locate."

"I can imagine," he said.  "Us, for instance.  We're not season ticket holders.  I'm assuming Shoop would have no way of knowing that we were there that night if you hadn't told him."

"True," she said.

"You know, Babe," he added, smiling with a nuzzle on her cheek.  "It's not your duty to solve every murder that occurs in Reardon."

"I know," she said.  "But this one seems so personal. That audio recording just seems to be calling to me like a beacon in the night.  You know, 'here I am, come get me'!"

"No, I don't know," he responded.

"And another thing," she said.  "I can't help thinking about the fact that we were there in the audience—so close to the victim when it happened.  Surely we must have seen or heard something."

"The 'heard something' would have been you—and your recording," he added.  "Not me.  For me, it was just a horrifying coincidence."

"We were so close," she mused.  "A few seats to our right, and we could have reached out and touched her."

"Her being the victim," he said with a cringe.

"Or her tea cup," she said, her eyes opening wide, turning to him.

"What?" he scowled.

"It just came back to me, something that Arliss said while she was sitting in the audience when we were there this afternoon," Pamela said.  "About the audience being so close to the stage."

"Yeah," he agreed.  "That was part of what made me so uncomfortable.  I felt like I was practically in the actors' laps."

"And one of the benefits of the audience being so close to the stage is that an audience member can just reach out and touch an actor—or prop.  Say, a tea cup."

"Are you suggesting that someone in the audience poisoned Belinda Purvis?" he asked.

"I think it's a distinct possibility," she replied, looking off in a sort of daze.  "Maybe you, yourself, couldn't have quite reached that little table, but the people next to you could.  And especially the people next to them."

"There was an old guy next to me, I remember," said Rocky.  "I think it was his wife next to him.  They looked harmless."

"What about the person on the other side of that couple?" she asked.

"I don't remember.  I think that was the end of the row.  There was just one person there."

"You're right," she noted.  "Silvus said the seats are numbered from one to ten in each row per quadrant. My seat was C6 and you were C7.  The couple next to us must have been C8 and C9, so that makes C10 a single patron on the end of the row."

"That person in C10 would have been in a really good position to reach the table, because it was set right there at the end of that row. I remember." He looked at her with excitement as they both seemed to realize that they might have stumbled onto a possibility.

"Now, let's not get carried away," she said.

"I'm not getting carried away!" he cried. "Babe, I may have just solved this murder!"

"You!" she exclaimed. "If anything, it's a joint effort. A Barnes and Barnes effort!" He gave her a resounding kiss and a little yelp too.

**CHAPTER 19**

The next day whizzed by. Pamela had three morning classes back to back and when she finally returned to her office, she barely had time to gulp down the BLT that Rocky had sent with her, before an onslaught of students peppered her with questions during the first of her scheduled office hours. Only now much later in the afternoon, did she have a chance to relax and put her feet up for a few minutes. She contemplated the soft goodness of her sofa. The cushions beckoned to her. It was always so pleasant to sip her tea and stretch out on her little couch.

"No!" she said out loud. Then realizing that anyone in the hallway might overhear her outburst, she quickly closed her mouth. She really wanted to look at the audio recording from the performance in her acoustic software, especially now that she had a rough idea what she might be listening—and looking—for. She turned to her computer monitor that was already on; a list of email addresses featured prominently. She quickly glanced down the list and determined that none of the messages were of any importance. Clicking out of her email program, she clicked on the acoustic analysis software icon on her desktop.

A screen popped into view showing an empty graph with vertical and horizontal axes. Pamela moved her cursor to the upper left-hand corner of the program and selected the recently added audio file from the play.  Immediately, a long series of jagged lines popped into the graph with a red vertical line running from the top of the graph to the bottom at the left side.  Pamela placed her cursor randomly on the jagged lines and the red line moved to the new location.  She then moved her cursor and clicked the 'play' button on the lower right hand corner of the screen.

Immediately from her computer's built-in speakers, the sounds of the play filled her room.  Using her cursor, she adjusted the volume with the on-screen volume control.  She listened a while, to determine exactly where in the recording she was.  The low volume music and the muffled sounds of many voices indicated that she was listening to the blackout at the end of the first scene.

*Yes*, she thought.  *This is the part I need to examine*.  Her expert ears listened as her equally expert eyes evaluated the shape and contour of the various jagged lines that quickly passed over the screen, the red vertical line indicating exactly when each sound was produced.  Soon the audience noises and the music faded.  There was a pause.  She assumed this had occurred when the house lights went down and the stage lights came up.  Then the second scene began.  She pushed the 'fast forward' button on her screen and ran the recording ahead until she located the scene between Joan and Belinda Purvis, as Lady Bracknell and Gwendolyn.  She listened carefully to this scene, paying particular attention to any ambient sounds such as a cup being set on a table or a spoon tapping the side of a cup.  It would have helped to have a video recording, she realized, so she could attribute each sound to its appropriate creator, but this audio recording would have to do.  At least, she had it.  And in her hands, it was probably a lot better than a video recording in the hands of the police.

Eventually, the moment arrived when Belinda Purvis began to react to the poison in the tea cup.  Pamela listened carefully to the sounds the young woman made.  She continued listening as the audience reacted with horror and the director came on stage and asked them to leave.  At this point, the recording ended.  She, of course, realized that she had ended it here when she had copied this segment to her computer from the original recording that she had given to Shoop.  She wondered what, if anything, Shoop was doing with it.  Or was he merely keeping it as evidence?  Expecting her to figure out what it meant, if anything?

As she had listened to the recording and looked at its acoustic output, she wrote down on paper the locations on the recording where various sounds occurred that she wanted to listen to again.  Now she returned her cursor to these specific spots and listened more closely, all the while looking at the jagged lines on her screen that indicated the nature of the sound being created.  The sound of voices created smooth, round lines.  The sound of mechanical things such as chairs being scraped over the floor created the sharp, jagged peaks.  Of course, there were many more features that she could extract from the shape, size, and variation of the lines on the screen.  But, much of her analysis was a process of elimination—trying to pair apparent sound from recording with matching visual output.  Her true detective skills came into play when she encountered a sound or a line feature that didn't seem to be accounted for logically in the audio recording.

She continued this procedure for several hours. Indeed, she lost track of time as she often did when she was totally engaged in acoustic research. Only, this time, she wasn't working on some scientific experiment that would conclude with the publication of a research article. This time she was attempting to solve a murder. She was certain that there must be some sound on this recording that would provide a clue to the murderer—how the poison was administered, who the killer was, where he was during the production—something. Her mind was open and she listened and looked for any small sound that seemed out of place.

Eventually she found it. During the blackout, amidst all of the music, audience mumbling and squirming, and set changing noises, she honed in on one sound that she couldn't identify. She played it again and again. It happened about mid-way through the blackout. It sounded like a short squeak. Then it was repeated again—the same sound, only slightly different. She replayed the recording and isolated the two noises. They were quite similar, almost identical, but slightly different. The first sound lasted six tenths of a second. Then there was a three second pause. Then the second sound occurred and it lasted seven tenths of a second. Obviously, the second sound was a bit longer; she wasn't certain why. She examined the acoustic output to see if she could locate the source of the sound. This would be a virtually impossible task. The output on her screen indicated variations in volume of the various sounds, but that could not be used to suggest that softer sounds were necessarily farther away and louder sounds were necessarily closer—unless, of course, you knew what the sounds were. Then, you could compare, let's say, the volume of the sound of a door opening and determine its approximate location based upon what a regular door opening would sound like at a certain distance from the recording device.

She listened again and again to the suspect sounds. Then, grabbing one of her handy-duty, miniature audio recorders—like the one she'd taken to the play—she flipped off her computer and headed out of her office.

Later as she was entering the Coffee Factory, she saw that the charming restaurant was again virtually empty. She moved into the darkened atmosphere, the sunlight filtering through the colored iron glass windows. She peered around for a waitress or—better yet—Silvus Barge, the person she actually wanted to see. She could hear the clinking of dishes in the kitchen off behind the staircase, through the curtained entrance. Standing at the hostess stand near the door, she glanced down at the counter where she could see a reservation book with very few slots marked for this evening. Further down the counter, another book was open to a printed image of the theater floor plan, showing each seat in the audience. She couldn't tell which date the page denoted, but there were large X marks placed on various seats. Surely, she thought, this wasn't the page for opening night, because that was a full house. This page must indicate the seats taken for another—later—night, now obviously cancelled because of Belinda Purvis's death.

As she leaned over the edge of the counter, she heard someone call out her name.

"Dr. Barnes!"

Looking up, she saw Silvus Barge come barreling through the kitchen entrance, wiping his hands on a towel.  He stuck the towel in his back pocket and hurried towards her, hand outstretched.

"We see you again so soon," he said, huffing, a huge smile barely visible under the massive puffs of hair that encased the lower part of his face.  "Are your friends returning too?"

"No, Mr. Barge…" she began.

"Silvus."

"Silvus," she said, "I actually returned because I'd like to go back upstairs to the theater and check out something that I noticed when I was here before."

"A clue, Dr. Barnes?" Barge asked, his eyes filled with curiosity and concern.

"Possibly," she replied.  "I won't know until I check." She stood there, her purse and jacket in hand, feeling much like a beggar.

"Come along!" he cried, gesturing and continuing towards the side stairs, with barely a change in his movement.  She trailed after him, scrounging around in her purse to extract her little audio recorder as she followed him up the rickety staircase.  When they arrived inside the theater, Barge flipped on the large overhead light that provided illumination but certainly no atmosphere.  He held open the maroon curtain and Pamela entered and moved immediately to Quadrant C where she and Rocky had been seated for the performance.

"Can I assist you with your experiment?" asked Barge, coming onto the stage area.

"You can," she replied.  "You can be my fake audience member."  She moved to the seat where she had sat during the performance, checking to be sure she had the right one by finding the C6 on the arm.

"How delightful!" said Barge. "A role I know well!"

"All I need you to do is sit in various seats here in this row while I record the sounds. I'll tell you when to sit and when to stand."

"At your service, my dear doctor," he answered, eagerly moving over to the front row next to her. She placed her belongings on the floor and pressed the play button on her tiny recorder.

"Test of audience seats," she said into the recorder's built-in speaker and then hit the stop button. "Silvus please sit here." She pointed to the seat labeled C8 which was the one the old gentleman who was seated next to Rocky had been in. Silvus squeezed his large frame into the chair.

"I hope this will work," he said sheepishly. "I may weigh a bit more than the average patron."

"You'll do just fine," she responded. "Now, when I point at you, stand up."

"That's all?" he asked.

"Yes," she said, "and when I point again, then sit back down."

Barge nodded and Pamela hit the 'play' button.

"Seat C8, rising," she said and then pointed at Barge. Following her direction, Barge lifted himself from seat C8 with only some difficulty. Pamela hit the stop button.

"Good," she said. "Now, we'll reverse it." She hit the 'play' button again' and said into the built-in mike, "Seat C8, sitting down." She pointed again and Barge sat back down in audience chair C8.

"Excellent!" she said to him. "Now, let's do the same thing with the next two seats." She motioned

Barge to seat C9, which was the same seat where the old gentleman's wife was seated during the performance, at least as Pamela could recall. She and Silvus Barge repeated the same routine with her announcing the seat number and the movement Barge was making—either rising or sitting.

"One more, if that's okay with you," she said and Barge moved to the last seat in the row, C10. They repeated the routine. This time when Barge rose and sat, there was a noticeable sound.

"I think the springs in this seat cushion need some oil," he chuckled. "Or maybe I just need to lose weight."

"They are a little squeaky," she replied, attempting not to give away the excitement she was feeling as she recorded the very same sound that she had identified on the actual performance recording—the sound that she had isolated as having occurred during the first blackout, right before Belinda Purvis collapsed and died on stage. She looked over at Silvus who had stood back up. She rose from her chair a few seats down from him. As she looked at him standing there, Silvus Barge was directly in front of the small white table where the actress had been seated at the fateful moment right before her death. In fact, he was just an arm's length away from her tea cup. It would have been a simple task, Pamela realized, for anyone in seat C10 to merely stand up, reach over and drop poison in Belinda's cup during the blackout and then sit back down. No one would be the wiser.

## CHAPTER 20

She crammed her little Civic into a much too small parking space behind Reardon City Hall. She probably should have looked for a larger spot along one of the downtown streets, but she was excited and in a hurry. It wasn't often that she actually felt anxious to talk to Shoop. The wind whipped her hair about, messing up her neat pageboy, but she was oblivious. Clutching her purse close to her chest—the mini-recorder bearing the new sounds inside—she dashed up the back steps faster than she'd ever taken them. Inside the old building, city workers and police officers moved about, efficiently going about their duties, ignoring her. She headed into the back entrance of the Reardon Police Department and went directly to Shoop's office which she knew was located near the back of the building. Through the glass partition that separated the top half of his office walls from the rest of the department, she could see Shoop entrenched behind his desk, bent over a folder, his nose virtually attached to the pages. Two officers were just exiting, almost bumping into her as she reached the door.

She knocked on the open door as she entered, hearing the soft whir of Shoop's humidifier humming in the corner. Shoop seemed to have a perennial cold— or asthma—she wasn't sure. He was never without his handkerchief and he always seemed to be dripping.

"Detective," she said, announcing herself in the doorway.

"Dr. Barnes," he replied, looking up, and standing at his desk with a sweeping gesture that she recognized was an invitation to enter, which she did. She headed for his chartreuse green plastic sofa that was covered with newspapers and package wrappers. Pushing aside the larger items of trash, she made a small spot for herself to sit. As soon as she sat, Shoop resumed his spot and closed the file on his desk.

"Did your buddy the mayor send you here to check on my progress on the Purvis case or do you have some information for me, Doctor?" he asked, ignoring Pamela's evident annoyance at his lack of housekeeping skills. Pamela was not a great cleaner, but at least she didn't leave trash on her chairs.

"Just possibly, Shoop," she replied, glancing around from the couch to a small waste can in the corner. It too was overflowing. She wondered if, when, anyone ever came in to clean this office. Shoop obviously didn't.

"Some clue on that audio recording?" he asked leaning back, now attentive, his elbows behind his massive head.

"Yes," she replied.

"Something one of the actors said or a sound they made?" he asked. "We've grilled that cast over and over—including your friend, Dr. Bentley. We can't find anyone with any sort of motive for wanting that young woman dead. Of course, they all had opportunity. Any one of them could have dropped that poison in her cup backstage. The problem is, why? None of them has the slightest reason to harm her. They all appear devastated. Although, your friend seems more upset that the play was cancelled than that that poor girl died."

"That's just Joan," said Pamela with a shrug. "She's really quite sweet." Why did she feel obligated to apologize for Joan?

"I'm sure," replied Shoop, wiping his long nose with his oversized hanky. "Anyway, none of the cast or crew—what there was of a crew; there were only two people working backstage—seem to have any animosity towards Belinda Purvis. So! Out with it! What do you have?"

"I absolutely agree with you about the cast," said Pamela, scrounging around in her large handbag on the sofa beside her. "It's good to hear that your investigation supports what I've come to believe."

"And that is?"

"That the killer was a member of the audience," she replied with a theatrical relish as she produced her little recorder, holding it high for him to see.

"Another recording?" he asked.

"I made this one less than an hour ago," she answered. "In the theater. Silvus Barge, the owner of the Coffee Factory had showed us—that is, me, Joan, and our friend Arliss—around the theater the other day and I got to thinking about the stage and its configuration. We noticed as we looked around that a person sitting in the audience could actually reach out and touch an actor or a stage prop if they were in the right seat. So today I returned to the theater and Silvus helped me recreate the sounds that an audience member would make if they were seated in various audience chairs."

"And how would that tell us who the killer is?" he asked, frowning. She could imagine the wheels turning in his large head.

"I recorded Silvus rising and sitting on several of the chairs that were nearest the table where Belinda Purvis was seated right before she collapsed that night. I made audio notations about which seat makes which sound. Then I compared the sounds on this recording to the sounds that were on the recording that I made during the actual performance with my acoustic software. I was particularly interested in sounds that occurred during the blackout, as I believe—as I suspect you do too—that if the killer was in the audience, he probably put the poison in Belinda's cup during the blackout right before her scene. I mean, he obviously couldn't have done it *during* the scene because all the people in the audience would see that."

"True," agreed Shoop, nodding his head. "So? What did you find?" His bushy eyebrows beckoned her to put up or shut up.

"Through a process of elimination, by knowing the actual sounds that each audience seat makes, I was able to determine exactly which seat I believe the killer was seated in the night of the performance. It was C10. That's the seat right on the end of the first row in the C quadrant. The sounds that seat makes when someone rises or sits in it are definitely audible during the blackout right before the scene when Belinda Purvis died."

"You say the sound made by this C10 seat is a sound you heard on the recording you made the night of the performance?"

"Yes," she replied. "Fortunately, or unfortunately for the killer, the seat he was in is a little squeaky—at least when someone rises from it or sits in it. Of course, that's not a problem during a performance because most audience members don't usually get out of their seats during a blackout. Most audience members realize that when the house lights go out and music plays that the scene is changing and they don't get up. If it were an intermission, the house lights would come up, and then everyone would probably get up. But in this instance, that didn't happen, so why would someone get out of their seat during a blackout?"

"Why indeed?" he asked, leaning forward onto his elbows. "How long did this little episode last? Do you have a record of that?"

"I do," she replied and reported quickly from her notes that were also in her purse the number of seconds that the audience member in C10 stood up during the blackout.

"That would be enough," he said, nodding.

"Enough?" she asked, as she crammed her notebook and recorder back into her purse.

"Time," he replied.

"So you think I'm right?"

"It's a definite possibility," he replied. "But it presents a problem."

"I know," she said, leaning back on the sofa and then sitting up abruptly as her back rubbed against something sticky. "How do we figure out who was in C10?"

"You were there, Dr. Barnes," he said, tapping his pencil on the manila file before him. "You're always so observant. Don't you remember who was seated in C10? Just where were you, by the way?"

"C6," she said sheepishly. Now why should she feel apologetic just because she didn't remember who was seated four seats down from her during a play? Did anyone really ever notice the people in surrounding seats during shows? She thought not.

"And your husband?"

"C7," she replied. "And, no, Shoop, he doesn't remember who was there either. Believe me, we've discussed this. There was an older couple in C8 and C9. The man was in C8 and his wife, I assume, was in C9. I really have no idea who was to their right. I'm guessing that if it was someone I knew, I would have spoken to that person when I sat down or when he sat down."

"It would be really helpful if you had some memory—any memory at all—of that person," said Shoop, tapping the desk with his hands sharply.

"I know, I know," she replied. "Believe me; I've racked my brain trying to remember who was in that seat. Obviously I saw the person, at least when I entered or left the theater. They must have been very nondescript."

"An appropriate thing for a murderer," he noted, hanky again wiping nose.

"I simply wasn't considering the people in the audience," she said. "My main focus was Joan. And Rocky, I guess. He was a bit annoyed about even being there."

"Dr. Barnes," Shoop said with a chuckle, "I thought your husband was an English teacher. Surely, he appreciates English drawing room comedies?"

"In a proscenium theater," she said with a shrug, "maybe. He hates to feel on display, as he describes it. He said he felt like the audience members on the opposite side of the theater were watching him.  He was very uncomfortable."

"You know," said Shoop, chewing the eraser on his stubby yellow pencil, "if they were watching him, they probably got a good view of our killer—just three seats down the aisle from your husband."

"Yes, that's true," she said.  "I remember the two people across from us who leaped up and went to Belinda when she collapsed."

"That would be her mother and her husband," he noted.  "They've been questioned thoroughly.  They told us they didn't notice anything unusual, but I will revisit them and ask specifically about any memory they might have of who was in seat C10.  It is an end seat, so that should make it easier for them to remember, I hope."

"If we just knew who was in C10," she mused.

"If," he said.

"You know, Shoop," she exclaimed.  "The theater may have a record of the person.  They do have records of season ticket holders and which seats they use for each production.  You could check that out."

"Hmm," he replied.  "No time like the present."  He stood up quickly, and motioned for her to follow him. Grabbing his wrinkled overcoat from a hook behind his door, he headed out of the office.  Pamela grabbed her purse, buttoned her jacket, and tripped quickly out behind him.

## CHAPTER 21

"Dr. Barnes!" greeted Silvus Barge, as Pamela and Shoop entered the Coffee Factory less than an hour after she had departed. "Back so soon?"  He came towards her, arms outstretched. "Oh, Detective! You too!  Have you found our killer?"  He clenched his pudgy hands together and brought them to his face.

"Sorry, Mr. Barge," replied Shoop. "Dr. Barnes and I would like to ask you a few more questions."

"Of course," replied the restaurateur, "I have answers.  Just probably not the ones you need."  He sighed and gestured for them to sit at one of the side booths.

"Actually," said Pamela, remaining standing, "Silvus, we'd like to discuss ticket sales for the production.  I noticed you keep a seating chart of the auditorium at the hostess stand up front.  I assume that's because you sell tickets there?"  She motioned for the threesome to move back to the counter near the entrance to the restaurant.

"We do," he replied, moving around behind the counter.  Shoop and Pamela stood side by side, arms resting on the edge, looking down at the items on the shelves below where Silvus was standing.  We train our wait staff to sell tickets for the shows.  They keep all the records here, but, to tell the truth, I'm not really sure how they do this.  Maybe I should get our business manager to explain things to you."

"That might be helpful," said Shoop, glancing at Pamela and then down at an array of papers, ledgers, and notebooks next to the cash register. Silvus raised a finger to them and then quickly headed into the back area behind the curtains under the stairs. Within seconds, he returned followed by a short, older woman with tight grey curls, glasses, and a no-nonsense demeanor.

"This is Dottie Ibberly," said Barge. "She's our business manager—and the person in charge of ticket sales for the theater." The sprightly lady sprinted past the owner and took up a defensive position behind the counter. "Dottie, Detective Shoop and Professor Barnes from Grace University."

"How do you do? Silvus tells me you have questions about ticket sales, Detective," she said, standing at attention, her hands folded almost protectively over the cash register.

"Dr. Barnes," said Shoop, gesturing to Pamela.

"Miss Ibberly," began Pamela, "I noticed the other day when I was in here that you kept a floor diagram of audience seats here at the cash register."

"Yes," said the woman. "I'm the business manager for the Factory which, believe me, keeps me mighty busy, but when Silvus asked me to take on the job of ticket sales for the little theater, I can't tell you how glad I was to do so! It simply breaks my heart, Detective, Dr. Barnes, to see what's happening to this wonderful old building. It's more than just a restaurant. It's a part of Reardon's past and its culture. It would be a catastrophe if it folded. Silvus knows how I feel."

Barge smiled warmly at Dottie Ibberly.

"I love this place and what it represents! I want it to succeed, and if bringing in this theater troupe will help give it a boost, then I am one hundred per cent behind that move."

"Dottie is being modest, Detective," said Barge. "She is more than just a supporter of the Coffee Factory. She's been with us since we opened. She's probably the best business manager around. If anyone can make two plus two equal five, it's Dottie. She's a financial genius—and organized!"

"There's no great honor in being organized, Silvus," scolded Dottie. Silvus Barge dropped his head like a school boy being chastised by a third grade teacher. "Everyone should be organized."

"Yes, Dottie," replied Silvus, "anyway, Dottie has developed a system for keeping track of ticket sales. It's not my area, so I'm not really sure what she does, but she can explain."

"Indeed," replied Dottie, sliding her glasses up her nose. Pamela almost expected to receive a blackboard lecture on proper penmanship from the neat little lady. "I don't know how most theaters do this, but obviously, a theater has to keep track of people who call to reserve tickets. The seats in the theater are all individually marked..."

"Yes," said Pamela, "we noticed this. That is one of the main concerns we want to discuss with you."

"What I do is simply maintain one chart of the audience seats for each performance night. When someone calls the restaurant to make a reservation, I write their name in pencil on the seats they choose for the appropriate night. If they don't care, I select appropriate seats for them and mark that in pencil on the appropriate seats. I always mark in pencil in case someone changes their mind and wants to change seats. When the seats are actually purchased, I mark through the paid for seat with a large X on the seat on the chart for that date."

"Makes sense," said Shoop, nodding. Pamela was glancing over the edge of the counter, looking at the ledger full of pages of floor plans of the audience seats.

"See," said Dottie Ibberly, noting Pamela's interest, "here's the floor plan for opening night." She set the ledger open on the counter edge and all four people could see the drawing of the stage floor and audience seats. All of the seats had large X's drawn through them. On many, Pamela could see that below each X were customer names. Dottie turned the ledger around so that Shoop and Pamela could get a better view of the floor plan.

"So, if someone reserves a seat or seats over the phone, you write in their name on a particular seat and when they pay for the ticket, you put an X over the seat."

"Correct, Detective," replied Dottie, smiling.

"Some seats don't have any names, only X's," said Pamela, looking carefully at the small print on the floor plan.

"Of course," said the woman. "Some people simply buy tickets here at the counter in advance of the show. But more likely, they purchase their seats at the door. That happened on opening night. We were not completely sold out in advance, but by the time the show began, we had a full house, as they say in theatrical parlance. So, many of our audience members bought tickets at the door."

"So, unfortunately," noted Shoop, looking over at Pamela, "you don't have any way to determine if a particular seat was sold in advance or bought at the door."

"Not if the audience member paid cash," said Dottie. "If they paid with a credit card, we could tell because when I process a credit card, I always indicate the seat numbers on the receipt."

"I notice," said Pamela casually, looking down at the chart, "that a lot of your reserved seats were in the front rows. For example, my husband and I were in C6 and C7. We had reserved seats that Joan had given us."

"Oh, yes, comp tickets," said Dottie. "We allowed each cast member a certain number of tickets for opening night to distribute to their friends." Pamela smiled at her. She wondered if she should feel guilty for not actually purchasing her tickets. Why? At least she was there with her husband doing her thing to support the new theatrical venture.

"Did you mark which of the seats were comp tickets?" asked Shoop.

"We do," replied Dottie. "See the little red C below the X. Then next to that you see Joan Bentley's name. We don't record who she gave the tickets to, but we do know that she was the one who gave out tickets for C6 and C7. Hmm, that's strange."

"What?" asked Pamela and Shoop together.

"It's strange that we gave Joan those particular seats. We should have given her C5 and C6."

"Why?" asked Pamela.

"To make even pairs in the first row," replied Dottie Ibberly, now staring intently at the floor plan for opening night. "Oh, yes, I remember. We sold that end seat to a single patron and that put off the count for the whole row in that section. Usually we try to steer individual ticket buyers to places where a group of three has already purchased seats. But someone bought C10 and that meant that couples were forced into C8 and C9 and then C6 and C7 and so on down the row. It's annoying but sometimes it happens. I believe we eventually solved it because—oh, yes! There was a single ticket buyer for C3! That solved that row. So there wasn't an empty seat in the first row! That would be horrible in such a tiny theater!"

"Horrible," agreed Pamela, looking at Shoop. His brain was obviously churning, as was hers.

"Ms. Ibberly," said the detective, "on your chart you have C10 marked with an X but no other information as you do with some of these other seats. I assume that means that the person who purchased C10 did so in person here in the restaurant or at the door?"

"No," she replied, "not at the door. As I said, whoever purchased C10 only bought the one ticket which forced us to scramble to sell at least one other seat in that row to a single ticket buyer to maintain a full row. I don't remember who purchased it, but I do know it was purchased soon after tickets went on sale."

"And not with a credit card?" asked Shoop.

"No," she said. "Otherwise I would have recorded that data on the chart. It must have been cash. And I don't know who sold it. It wasn't me, although I don't personally sell many tickets. They're generally sold by the wait staff or the hostess on duty."

"Would your hostesses remember who sold the ticket?" suggested Pamela.

"Our hostesses are all of our waiters and waitresses," said Barge. "They all take turns serving that position."

"And they all know how to take ticket reservations," added Dottie.

"All fifteen of them," said Barge.

"I don't suppose any of them ever mentioned to either of you," said Shoop, "that they had sold this one ticket at the end of this front row for the opening night performance, did they?"

"No," replied Dottie.  "It's not a crime, detective! It's much better to sell one ticket than not sell any ticket at all.  I would surely not chide any of our staff for doing so."

"No, of course not," said Pamela.  She looked at Shoop and he looked disappointed.

"Detective," said Barge, looking back and forth from Pamela to Shoop, "do you think the killer was in C10? Is that why you're so keen on determining who bought that ticket?"

"Oh, no!" cried Dottie.  "You think someone in the audience, in this seat, is the one who killed poor Belinda!   I thought, I hoped that maybe it was someone from outside who, who..."

"We don't know for sure," said Shoop.

"At the moment, Dottie," said Pamela with a hand on the elderly woman's hand, "it's all conjecture.  We think it's possible that someone sitting in C10 might have been able to place the poison in Belinda's cup. Now, we just need to try to find out who was sitting there."

"I understand," she said, shaking her head as she looked around at the trio of people staring at her.  "Oh my, I wish my little system could provide you with the answer you need.  I wish now I had trained my waiters and waitresses to ask each ticket buyer for their name. That would certainly have solved this terrible crime!"

"You couldn't have known," said Pamela, consoling her. "And besides, if the killer knew he was going to poison Belinda when he purchased the ticket, he'd just give you a fake name."

Eventually, when it was clear that no additional information would be forthcoming from the Coffee Factory's business manager, and when Shoop had double checked the names and numbers of all of the establishment's staff for further questioning, Pamela and Shoop left, their questions only partially answered.

## CHAPTER 22

Exhausted now from a long walk around their neighborhood with Candide, the tiny dog obviously having much more energy than she did, Pamela plopped herself like a giant boulder in her favorite green arm chair in her bedroom and flung her feet onto the matching ottoman in front.

"Goodness, Candide," she panted, "where do you get your pep? I thought fifteen dog years made you an old man in people years! You practically sprinted around our block!" Candide agreed with her assessment of his prowess by leaping up on her knees, demanding additional attention. "No! Get down and relax! I—I mean you—need to relax after that work-out!" Candide whimpered, but relented and pawed out a prone position next to the ottoman, and placed his tiny head on top of his tiny paws. He looked for all the world like a little sphinx surveying all the major events that were happening around the bedroom. "Good boy!" she cried. Candide panted more slowly, obviously recovering from the strenuous walk much faster than his mistress.

Pamela reached for the local newspaper that was lying beside her feet on the ottoman. She opened the little daily paper to a second page photo spread about Belinda Purvis. *Oh, no!* she thought, *this really is getting major local attention. Poor Joan!* She perused the page full of photographs of the young victim.

Some pictures were of Belinda Purvis in her character costume for the production. These were obviously publicity photos taken before opening night. Pamela saw Joan in one of the pictures, seated across from Belinda holding up the tea pot over Belinda's deadly tea cup. Other photographs she hadn't seen. There was one of Belinda with her husband Matt that appeared to have been taken at their wedding. A headshot of the young woman at a younger age was no doubt from a high school or college yearbook. In this picture, Belinda was still recognizable but her hair was styled quite differently and she looked a lot younger.

*How sad,* thought Pamela. *Such happy pictures to mark such a sad event.* And to have them plastered all over the newspaper. She wondered how Belinda's family must feel to see this homage to her following her tragic death. Reporters, she realized, were not concerned with the feelings of the people they described; they were only concerned with getting the story. *Usually this is a good thing*, she mused, *particularly if it helps solve the murder.* But she speculated on the wisdom of how publishing all these photographs of Belinda would aid in tracking down her killer. Obviously the killer knew what she looked like. None of the information or photographs, as she could tell, would provide readers with any guide to helping the police track down the killer.

*No*, she thought. *What they needed to do was to report in the newspaper that the killer was sitting in C10.* If anyone remembered who was in that seat, they should report it to the police. Then, just as suddenly, she thought, *stupid, Pamela! If you tell the whole town where the killer was seated the night of the play, not only will all of the audience know, the killer will know too. He'd probably skip town, never to be seen again. That wouldn't help the police.* No, she realized, *it's best to leave things the way they are. Keep this information about knowing—or at least being somewhat certain—where the killer was seated during the performance quiet.* That's obviously what the police—Shoop—were doing. If word got out about their suspicions, they'd probably lose any chance of capturing the culprit.

Candide made a little snort. He'd apparently fallen asleep. *Lucky fellow*, she thought. *Wouldn't it be nice to be a dog and not have to worry about murderers?* She allowed herself to drift off, the open newspaper falling across her face. Suddenly, the paper was snatched from her and flung onto the bed.

"Rocky!" she cried, looking up, rubbing her eyes. Her big, burly husband was standing in front of her, ladle in hand, his arms crossed in annoyance.

"You're sleeping!" he cried.

"Just a little nap," she squeaked. "I'm exhausted. Candide dragged me up one street and down another. He's relentless."

"Yes, I see," said Rocky, nodding. "He's a regular task-master. You must have lost ten pounds on that little outing."

"From your mouth to God's ear," she whined, jerking herself up in her soft chair. "Is supper ready? I'm starving."

"I can imagine, after that long, demanding walk," he said, smiling and nodding. "You were gone over...ten minutes!"

"Ten minutes!" she exclaimed. "It seemed like ten hours!"

"Candide is obviously in better shape than you," he chuckled.

"He is not," she pouted. "Look, he's totally wiped out!" She motioned to Candide, who at the mention of his name, leaped up and began jumping in the air.

"Sure," said Rocky, patting the poodle on the top of his fuzzy head when he was air bound. "Totally wiped out!"

"Don't be mean, Rocky," she said. She pushed the newspaper article on the floor and scooted up in the chair.

"What's in the paper?" he asked, noting that she had obviously been looking through it. The second page was folded back against the first and then folded over again on itself.

"Oh, a big pictorial on Belinda Purvis," she said.

"The poisoning victim," he clarified.

"Yes. Photographs from the production and some from her wedding. Also what appears to be a high school or college yearbook picture."

"No talk about the killer?" he asked.

"Nope," she said. "Guess the police are keeping this one close to their vests."

"You mean they have a lead," he said.

"Yes," she replied, "but you didn't hear it from me. It looks like the killer was not a cast or crew member."

"Someone from outside?"

"No," she said, staring at him, "someone in the audience."

"Oh, my God!" he cried. "They don't suspect you, do they?"

"Me?" she howled. "Why on earth would they suspect me? I didn't even know the woman!"

"So who then?"

"I can't believe you would think I'd kill someone."

"I don't believe you would."

"But you think the police might think I would!"

"No," he said, "I just think they might think you're clever enough to pull off something like this."

"Is that some sort of left-handed compliment?" she answered. "For that matter, you were in the audience too. You're pretty clever. Maybe you did it!"

"Whoa! Wait a minute!" he admonished her. "You've got the wrong idea here. I'm not suggesting that you did it or that the police even have a reason to think you did it. I'm not suggesting anything!"

"Then don't say so!"

"Okay, okay," he said, sitting down beside her on the ottoman. Candide, who had perked up during this potential battle, now settled back into a relaxed position on the floor. "I'm sorry. I just don't know anyone else who happened to be there that night. Who do they think did it?"

"C10," she said.

"Oh, yeah," he said. "The audience theory."

"Yes," she repeated. "The person sitting in seat C10."

"Great! And how are they—you—certain of this?"

"It's mostly a process of elimination," she said, "and—my acoustic analysis." She smiled broadly and puffed her chest out a bit.

"So," he said looking intently into her eyes. "What did you do?"

"I didn't do anything, Rocky! I simply listened to the audio recording of the production and then compared some unusual sounds on it with the sound made by the audience chairs closest to the table where Belinda Purvis was poisoned."

"Sounds?"

"Yes!" she said proudly. "The seat labeled C10 makes a very distinctive squeak when someone sits in it or rises from it. That sound definitely occurs on the audio recording of the production—during the blackout."

"So let me get this right," he said, attempting to follow her story. "You know that someone who was seated in this particular seat actually stood up and sat down during the blackout right before Belinda Purvis died?"

"Yes."

"And this C10 seat is—as I recall—close to the table where Belinda was seated on stage?"

"Directly in front of it," she replied. "Actually, I think the police would have eventually begun to suspect this possibility. My determination of the sound made by C10 during the blackout, I think, just solidified their thinking and focused their suspicions on this unknown audience member."

"Do they have any idea who the person might be?" he asked.

"The Coffee Factory does keep records of ticket sales," she said, "but only if a buyer makes a reservation in advance. Anyone who buys a ticket in person at the Factory or at the door on the night of the performance will not have their name recorded. That's the way it was with the person who purchased the ticket for C10 on opening night."

"Too bad," he noted.

"Yes," she said. "But they haven't given up. At least they know where the killer was seated. There are other ways of determining who was sitting in that seat. I'm sure they're looking into them."

"C10 was close to where we were," he said.  "I mean, we were seated pretty close to that little table where that woman was when she collapsed."

"I know," said Pamela.  "You remember that I was in C6 and you were in C7."

"So I was closer to the killer than you."

"Yes, you were.  Do you remember anything about who was sitting there?"

"I remember the little old couple sitting next to me. They were cute."

"They were C8 and C9."

"Yeah," he said, scrunching up his face as he actively tried to recall the audience members seated next to him the night of the fateful performance.

"Do you remember anything about the person in C10?" she asked.

"I'm thinking," said Rocky.  He closed his eyes shut and rocked back and forth, his ladle tapping an unknown rhythm on his shoulder.  "I think, I think...the little old lady may have said something to the person."

"She spoke to the killer?" asked Pamela with excitement.

"She seemed very outgoing," he said.  "You know, the type of person who speaks to strangers in elevators."

"Yes," said Pamela.  "Not like you."

"And rightly so," he said, "the person sitting next to her was a murderer!"

"She didn't know it," said Pamela.  "She was just being friendly."

"Sometimes being friendly can be deadly."

"Oh, Rocky," said Pamela in frustration.  "I doubt that little old lady was in any danger from that killer.

The person obviously was determined to kill Belinda Purvis—and no one else."

"Who knows?" asked Rocky. "The little old lady might have annoyed the killer and the killer would have done her in too."

"Ridiculous!" cried Pamela. "I doubt that he'd do that!"

"*He* couldn't do that," said Rocky, with a sudden smile.

"What?" she asked, looking at his Cheshire cat grin. "Do you remember something? Why couldn't he kill the old lady next to him? What do you remember? Out with it!"

"*He* couldn't kill her—because he was a *she*!"

## CHAPTER 23

"The killer was a woman," was a mantra repeating over and over in Pamela's mind throughout the next day and she now continued to contemplate it on her office couch.  Of course, she didn't know this for a fact.  Rocky wouldn't swear to the fact that the person in the seat next the elderly couple on his right was definitely female, but he seemed fairly certain that she was.  Pamela wondered if Rocky's hunch was enough information to work with.  Should she contact Shoop?

Her musings were cut short when Samantha appeared at her door, her thesis notes and records held in front of her like a prayer book.

"Dr. Barnes?" she said in a wee voice. "I know I don't have an appointment, but could you please take a look at some of my statistical outputs?  I've been running correlations on my two subject groups and the results I'm getting just don't make sense."  She clutched the stack of papers pitifully, some of them slipping out of the pile.  Pamela wondered if lack of organization might be at least one of the causes of Samantha's problems.  Of course, she didn't express this thought as the girl had just lost her friend.  The very fact that she was back at work was a positive sign.

"Sam," said Pamela, gesturing for her flustered-looking student to enter and have a seat next to her on the couch.  Samantha removed her backpack and deposited it on the floor and plopped down beside her teacher.

"Here," she said, flinging the messy stack of papers onto Pamela's lap. Pamela smiled and glanced down at the statistical output charts for Sam's thesis project. She was intimately familiar with this study, as she was with all of her thesis advisees' work. She peered at the columns and rows of numbers on the first page and moved to the next page, first checking the heading.

"See," said Samantha, "the correlations are practically non-existent for my two groups in the first condition, and then, they're negative in the second condition! Dr. Barnes! Why would that be? I must be doing something wrong!"

Pamela continued to glance at Sam's work, not only the computer output of her statistical tests, but also referring back to Sam's thesis manuscript on the bottom of the stack of papers which delineated the hypotheses for her various tests. She quickly refreshed her memory of the five or six hypotheses and sub-hypotheses that Sam had set forth in her thesis proposal and then turned back to the loose pages of output that indicated whether or not her findings confirmed these.

"Did I do something wrong with the tests?" asked Sam, her face a mask of horror, "or do I just not have any valid hypotheses? Oh, my God! I'll never graduate if all of my hypotheses are disconfirmed!"

"Now, Sam," said Pamela gently, her hand on the young woman's shoulder, "we would never do that to you. If your hypotheses are all truly unconfirmed— and that's a big if—you'll simply have to determine why that happened and defend your argument to your committee. Believe me, it's happened before. But, let's not jump the gun. As I'm looking at your printouts, I think there's actually a much simpler explanation for your findings. Look here. How did you enter these data? It looks like your independent variable got entered as your dependent variable in this test."

Sam peered at the printout. Her finger moved over the small chart on the page.

"Oh, my God, Dr. Barnes, you're right!" she gasped. "That probably screwed up all the rest of the tests too!"

"It probably did," agreed Pamela. "I bet if you run your data again and just switch these groups around like they should be, you'll get the results more in line with what you hypothesized."

"I can do that," she cried. "Oh, my! That will surely be easier than starting from scratch and collecting all new data—or worse, having no significant findings at all! I just can't imagine how I managed to make such a stupid error!" She sat staring at the paper, shaking her head.

"Well, you've been mighty distracted," said Pamela gently. "Your friend just died. It's certainly understandable that you'd find it difficult to concentrate on school work."

"I thought I had things under control," said Sam, her shoulders shaking, a sob escaping from her lips. "I thought if I focused on my thesis, Dr. Barnes, I'd be able to forget about what happened to Belinda. But I guess I just can't. This just proves it. I'm an idiot." Pamela saw a tear form and then suddenly drip down the side of her student's face.

"You probably tried to get back to your studies too soon," suggested Pamela. "It's difficult to cope with a death. And when it's the death of a young person, it's worse, I think. I mean, we expect our grandparents to die and that's sad, but you surely don't expect one of your high school friends to die at her age, and in such a horrible way."

"I know," agreed Sam, shaking her head and gathering her papers together. Clutching them to her chest, she said, "I can't forget about it. Gee, Dr. Barnes, I just went to her funeral the other day. It was so sad. You should have seen her mother—Mrs. Whatley. I don't think I've ever seen her look so miserable. Like she could barely walk. There were several people who had to help her get in and out of the church. I've been spending a lot of time at her house—when I wasn't running my data. She was almost like a second mother to me when Belinda and I were kids. I wish there was more I could do to help her."

"Maybe there is," said Pamela. "Maybe the best thing you can do for Belinda's mother now, Sam, is to help find her daughter's killer. I certainly can't imagine how horrible I would feel if anyone harmed—let alone killed—my daughter. I know I would do everything in my power to track down the person though."

"Of course I would do that if I could," said Sam, "but I don't have any idea who killed Belinda. Neither does her Mom."

"She's never said anything to you about anyone she might suspect?" asked Pamela.

"Not really," said Sam. "Belinda is—was—a really nice person. She just didn't have any enemies. Her husband Matt is super and his family is great. I can't see anyone hurting her. I just can't."

"And yet..." said Pamela.

"I know," said Sam.  "Maybe that's why I messed up my data.  It's more than just Belinda dying.  That's bad enough.  But there's nothing I can do about it now.  I can't bring her back.  But this person, this maniac who killed her.  He's out there and nobody knows who he is.  Who knows why he did this to Belinda?  Will he hurt somebody else?  Oh, Dr. Barnes, I guess I am dwelling on this, even though there's not really much I can do about it."

"Maybe you can," she said.  "You knew Belinda really well.  You know her mother well too.  Maybe there's something somewhere in Belinda's past—or even present—that would provide a clue to the killer's identity.  There might be someone out there who had it in for Belinda for some strange reason that no one's aware of.  It certainly appears that this killer was targeting Belinda; it didn't appear to be a random poisoning.  At least, that's what the police are saying."

"I know," said Sam.  "That's what's so strange.  Why?  She was so happy.  In a happy marriage.  In that play.  She was really just having a wonderful time of her life."

"Had there been any—not so wonderful times?" asked Pamela.

"Not really," said Sam, squinting her eyes as if trying to remember something.  "She was pretty popular in high school.  But, Dr. Barnes, she was never stuck-up.  You know, how some girls are at that age."

*Yes*, Pamela thought, she did know some high school girls could be very mean.  Her daughter, Angela, had experienced some particularly virulent ones in her young life.

"Maybe it was because her mother was always warning her about mean girls," said Sam somewhat wistfully.

"Mean girls?" asked Pamela.

"Yes," said Sam, "I remember her mother always telling Belinda to watch out for the mean girls. Belinda usually just laughed. When I asked her once what her mother was talking about, she'd just waved her hand and said her mother was over protective. It never came up again. But I always remember Mrs. Whatley saying that and thinking how strange it was."

"Maybe her mother knew something that Belinda didn't," suggested Pamela.

"Or that Belinda didn't want to know," said Sam, looking suddenly and directly at her professor.

"I'm curious, Sam," said Pamela. "I believe you said that Belinda's mother was at the play opening night? I mean, she witnessed what happened to her daughter?"

"Oh, Dr. Barnes, yes!" cried Sam, now succumbing again to sobbing. "I wish she hadn't been there. I wish she hadn't seen that! Matt was there with her. They were both right in the front row is what I hear."

"Because you weren't there?" asked Pamela.

"I had to work," said Sam. "I planned to go the next night. I really wish I'd been there the first night and that Belinda's mother hadn't been there. How horrible for her to witness that happen to her daughter."

"I was there, as you know," said Pamela. "I saw it all, of course. It was horrible. I believe I know who Belinda's mother and husband are. I remember a woman and a young man seated directly across from us. They both leaped up and rushed onto the stage when Belinda collapsed."

"I'm sure that was them."

"Did you ever ask Mrs. Whatley about what she saw during the play? Did she see anything that she thought would help the police?"

"I don't think so," said Sam. "I know they questioned her, but she was so focused on Belinda and what was happening to her, that was really all she said."

"I wonder about those mean girls she spoke about?" questioned Pamela.

"Yes?"

"I wonder if she saw any of them at the performance?" asked Pamela, almost to herself.

"If they even exist," offered Sam. "But, no, she never said anything about them being at the show. Dr. Barnes, do you think one of these mean girls that Belinda's mother warned her about years ago might be the one who poisoned her?"

"I don't know," said Pamela, "but the police evidently aren't having much success in tracking the killer, so they may appreciate any sort of trail we might provide them."

"You can surely do that, Dr. Barnes!" exclaimed Sam. "You've solved so many crimes, I've heard. I'm sure you'll be able to figure out who killed Belinda!"

"Let's not get ahead of ourselves here, Sam," said Pamela. "First steps first."

"Dr. Barnes," said Sam eagerly, "let me help you! If you think there's a way to track down the person who killed Belinda, let me help you do it!"

"You can help me," said Pamela thoughtfully, standing and moving over to her desk. "Since you and Belinda were such good friends—and since you're also so close to her mother, you can help me by introducing me to Mrs. Whatley.  Can you do that?"

"Oh, yes!" cried Samantha, rising with excitement. "Do you want me to call her?  Or do you just want her phone number so you can call her?   I have it memorized."

"Why don't you just write it down here," said Pamela, motioning to a scratch pad on her desk.  Sam moved over and grabbed the pen that Pamela handed her and quickly jotted down the phone number.

"Do you want me to call Mrs. Whatley for you?" she asked.

"No," said Pamela firmly, sitting at her desk and picking up the telephone receiver.  "I want you to go and rerun your data."   She pointed to the pile of papers lying forlornly on the couch.  Sam smiled and gathered the wayward sheets together.  With a cheery smile, she headed out of the office.

## CHAPTER 24

She stared at the number on the square piece of yellow paper. Before she sat at her desk, she walked over to her door and gently pressed it shut. Then she headed back and carefully sat in her desk chair, gathering her—what? Thoughts? Strength? What could she say to a woman who had just lost her daughter to a murderer right in front of her eyes? She pressed the numbers on her telephone. Almost immediately, the phone was answered. A woman's voice spoke anxiously.

"Hello."

"Mrs. Whatley?" she said tentatively.

"Yes, this is Leticia Whatley," said the soft voice.

"Mrs. Whatley," said Pamela, "Samantha Landry gave me your number. Please forgive my forwardness in calling you. I know this is a difficult time..."

"Who is this?" the woman interrupted.

"Oh, excuse me. My name is Pamela Barnes. Dr. Pamela Barnes from the Psychology Department at Grace University. I'm Sam's academic and thesis advisor..."

"Oh, of course," said the voice on the other end. "I know who you are, Dr. Barnes. I've read about your work with the local police department in the newspaper. Oh, my God! Are you helping them find Belinda's killer?"

"I, uh, I," Pamela stammered.  Leticia Whatley certainly did get right to the point.

"Oh, I hope you are!" she cried.  "They haven't found that maniac who killed my daughter! They don't even seem to have a clue!"  Pamela could hear her hysterical sobs over the phone.

"Mrs. Whatley," she began, trying to sound calm.  "I guess you might say that I am assisting the police in my capacity as an acoustics technology expert.  I'm wondering if I might ask you some questions."  Of course, she didn't mention that the police had not sanctioned this call nor even suggested it.  It was Leticia Whatley that had merely jumped to her own conclusion.

"Oh, Dr. Barnes," she said, "please ask me anything. I'll do anything I can to help you find whoever did this to Belinda!  I still can't believe it.  I just can't believe she's gone.  It was so horrible.  She looked so beautiful and she did such a wonderful job.  You know, she'd been in a few plays in high school, but nothing since then.  This was so exciting for her—and for Matt."

"Matt is her husband?" Pamela asked, even though she knew the answer.

"Yes," replied Leticia Whatley.  "We were both there at the theater when, when…"

"Actually, Mrs. Whatley," said Pamela, "so was I. My husband and I were in the audience too.  My colleague Joan Bentley had asked us to attend…"

"Oh, yes," interjected Leticia, "Dr. Bentley! Belinda liked her so much!  She was such a nice woman, Belinda told me.  You were there, Dr. Barnes? You saw what happened to my Belinda?"

"Yes," replied Pamela gently.  "My husband and I were seated in the front row, actually fairly close to the little table where your daughter was seated when..."

"Oh," said the woman, "yes, I believe I remember seeing you. I couldn't help but look at the people seated across from us. I remember there was an elderly couple sort of behind the table. Then another younger couple—or they seemed like a couple—next to that couple. I remember that the man acted as if he wasn't too happy to be there. He was scowling a lot."

"That was my husband, Rocky," said Pamela, "and you're right. He was a bit annoyed with having to be there. Mostly he disliked sitting in the front row where people could stare at him. I guess he was right to be concerned. You evidently did notice him."

"I'm sorry, Dr. Barnes," she said. "Your husband is very striking. It's hard not to notice him. He's quite attractive. Oh, excuse me, I shouldn't say that."

"It's fine," said Pamela, laughing. "I feel the same way. He can cook too, by the way."

"Then don't let him slip away," she scolded the professor over the phone.

"Don't worry. Mrs. Whatley, you are remarkably observant. I'm surprised the police haven't been doing more to pick your brain."

"Oh, they've been trying," she replied with a sigh. "They asked me to try to remember anything or anyone I saw who seemed out of place, but I wouldn't know what was out of place because I've never been to that theater before. It might be different if I'd attended a rehearsal, but I hadn't. So I don't know what I'd be looking for."

"Did they ask you about people in the audience?" asked Pamela.

"The audience?" she repeated. "No. Is there someone in the audience who is a suspect, Dr. Barnes? I thought the police thought the killer put the poison in Belinda's cup backstage. I thought they believed that it was a cast member or someone on the crew—or maybe someone who had slipped in from outside and put the poison in the cup when it was on the prop table. Those were some of the things they seemed interested in. Of course, I wouldn't know about those things because I wasn't backstage and Belinda hadn't really talked to me about things that went on backstage. She mostly just talked about the play and her character and the other actors and the scenes she had with them."

"I see," said Pamela. And she did. The police probably didn't consider the victim's mother a likely source of valuable information. "What about the audience?"

"You mean did I see anyone in the audience do anything suspicious?" Leticia asked.

"That," agreed Pamela. "Or—did you recognize anyone in the audience?"

"Not really," she replied.

"What does that mean?" asked Pamela. "Was there someone in the audience who looked familiar?"

"I recognized people—or thought I recognized people—in the audience. I'm guessing some of those people are well known in Reardon. It was opening night and I know that it was an important event for the downtown community and for Reardon as a whole. Of course, the mayor wasn't there. I think Belinda and the whole cast were hoping he'd be there. He's been such a supporter of the group."

"Actually," said Pamela, "he'd planned to be there. I recently spoke to him and he was planning to attend one of the next performances."

"Oh, that's good," she said, and then her voice saddened, "not that it matters now. Belinda is gone. Nothing matters now."

"I think it would matter to Belinda," suggested Pamela, "that we find her killer."

"You're right," said Leticia, pulling in a sob. "I can't let myself lose control. I have to hold it together for her. I have to do what I can to find this monster!"

"Mrs. Whatley—Leticia," Pamela whispered. "Can you think back to that night. Think back to when you were sitting in the theater before the play began, just looking around the place, looking at all the people sitting there waiting for the show to commence. You said you remembered my husband sitting in the front row across from you. I was sitting next to him, on his left. I guess that would be your right as you looked across at us. You also said you remembered an elderly couple on my husband's right, your left."

"Yes," she replied. "I remember them. They were a cute little old couple. So obviously still in love. They held hands during the blackout."

"You could see them during the blackout?" Pamela asked.

"Well, no," she replied, "but I noticed that he grabbed her hands as the lights started to fade."

"You're remarkably observant," said Pamela. "What about the person seated next to them?"

"You mean in the aisle seat?"

"Yes, right on the aisle where the actors made entrances and exits."

"Right behind where Belinda was seated," Mrs. Whatley said, her voice filled with awe.

"Yes," noted Pamela. "Do you remember anything about the person in that seat?" She was careful not to suggest to Leticia Whatley that the seat was occupied by a woman as Rocky had remembered. She wanted to get the victim's mother's reaction firsthand. And, as Dottie Ibberly at the Coffee Factory did not have that seat marked as having been reserved by anyone, season ticket holder or otherwise, then the person obviously purchased the ticket in advance with cash or right at the door.

"Let's see," said Leticia. "She looked a bit like Ruth Fenton, I remember thinking."

"She?" asked Pamela. "It was a woman in the seat?"

"Yes," replied Leticia. "A young woman, blonde, if I recall. And, as I said, she looked a bit like Ruth Fenton. But Ruth was a brunette. She was a girl that Belinda used to know."

"One of her friends?" asked Pamela.

"Oh, no!" exclaimed Leticia Whatley. "Definitely not a friend. Ruth was more like an enemy—a mean girl. She and Belinda never got along. But I thought she moved away when Belinda went to college. At least, Belinda never mentioned Ruth Fenton again."

"You say she was mean," said Pamela, proceeding slowly. Here was the term she had heard just recently from Samantha Landry about this very phrase being said by Belinda's mother. A phrase that had confused her.

"Mrs. Whatley," began Pamela, "just how—why do you label this...Ruth Fenton...as a mean girl?"

"It was because of the way she treated Belinda in high school," said Leticia. "She and some of her friends, although I think she was the ring leader. She picked on Belinda. I don't know why. Belinda swore she never did anything to prompt her nasty behavior. I often wondered if Belinda was telling the truth. I mean, Dr. Barnes, all kids can be mean. All kids can be bullies if given half a chance, but that just wasn't how Belinda was. I never saw her do anything like that; I never heard about her doing any kind of cruel behavior from her friends, or neighbors, or school officials, or teachers, or anybody! If she'd ever given Ruth Fenton and her pals a reason to pull pranks and...well, I just don't think she did."

"Pranks?" asked Pamela.

"Yes," said Leticia. "Mean pranks. Ruth Fenton and a few other girls seemed to revel in making Belinda miserable. They did ridiculous things like putting bugs in her lunchbox, or writing nasty notes to the teachers and signing Belinda's name. They really liked to get her in trouble. Luckily, most of Belinda's teachers never believed that she would do the things that Ruth Fenton set her up for. Invariably, her pranks backfired. And, Dr. Barnes, Belinda never retaliated against Ruth. Never! I don't know why. I don't think I could have put up with all of that harassment from those mean girls. But she did. I don't know. Maybe they liked to pick on her because she was so forgiving and didn't let their nasty stunts get to her. It all just seemed to float off of her back. Her mind was always occupied with positive things—exciting things. Eventually, Ruth Fenton and her cohorts just gave up and went away. I guess. At least, I hoped that's what happened. Maybe not."

"Maybe not," said Pamela in a hushed voice. "Maybe not. Do you know what happened to her after high school?"

"No, and now that it's beginning to look as if she might have had something to do with..."

"Let's not jump to conclusions," said Pamela quickly. "This Ruth Fenton might not have anything at all to do with Belinda's killer. But it would be helpful if we could locate her."

"Oh, Dr. Barnes, I'm so sorry I don't know where she went or where she might be." Pamela could hear another sob forming.

"It would certainly help if we had a photograph of Ruth Fenton."

"Oh!" cried Leticia. "That's easy! I have all of Belinda's high school yearbooks. I'm sure Ruth is in them."

## CHAPTER 25

After speaking with Belinda Purvis's mother, Pamela immediately phoned Detective Shoop and clued him in on the possibility that the person who was seated in C10 and who had the best opportunity to place the poison in the young victim's cup looked a lot like a woman she had known throughout her childhood and who had tormented her mercilessly in high school. She suggested that Shoop send an officer to the Whatley house and pick up one or more of Belinda Purvis's high school yearbooks and find the photograph of Ruth Fenton. Shoop thanked her and said he'd send someone to collect the yearbooks right away.

When she hung up, she realized that although she had done the right thing in alerting the police to the possibility that this Ruth Fenton might be the killer and that her photograph might be in some old yearbooks, she herself had no idea what the murder suspect looked like. She was chiding herself for not running immediately over to the Whatley house and grabbing the yearbooks herself, but this thought was wedged in between reacting to the line of students outside her office door. There was an upcoming exam in her intro class and good students and bad students alike were beginning to get worried—as they typically did right before a test—and so they invaded her office asking for individual help in preparing for the day of reckoning. She was more than happy to help them—

'help' being the operative word. Some seemed to want to know the actual questions on the exam. She wasn't about to go that far and she knew all the tricks that devious students used to secure information from unsuspecting professors. The afternoon had dwindled away and the line was still long.

As one tall young man who looked as if he should be on the football team if he wasn't already left her office, demoralized that she wouldn't give him a copy of last year's exam (just to study), the next student in the apparently growing line popped in.

"Sam!" she exclaimed. "You're back so soon! What a pleasant surprise! I'd much rather chat about your thesis than fend off all these attempts from freshmen to get special hints about their mid-term tomorrow. Don't tell me you've already run all that data again!"

"Hi, Dr. Barnes," said Samantha Landry, entering and placing herself on the student-designated chair by the doorway. She looked definitely brighter than earlier. *Obviously*, thought Pamela, *the problem with the data analysis was solved.* She was clutching a big red bound book.

"More stat problems?" she asked.

"No," said Samantha, smiling. "I brought you something."

"Not something to grade I hope," said Pamela with a mock cowering gesture. "Or critique?"

"Nope," said the young woman. "Belinda's mom called me a little bit ago. She told me about your call and, Dr. Barnes, she's so grateful to you. To have you take such an interest in Belinda and in trying to find out who did this to her..." Her voice broke and she started to cry. She rubbed a tear with the back of her hand.  "She told me that she told you about the mean girls and about this one girl named Ruth Fenton."

"Do you remember this Ruth Fenton, Sam?" asked Pamela.

"Only vaguely," she said with a shrug, "and I really wish I could remember her more because I want to help find the person who did this to Belinda!"  She squeezed her lips together.  "Anyway, Mrs. Whatley definitely remembers her because she bothered Belinda so much.  Belinda was very good about pretending that she wasn't bothered by this, I guess, because I knew her all throughout elementary school and high school and I can't remember her mentioning being bothered by any girls."

"Sometimes kids can be terrible bullies and the tragedy is that the victim is often too afraid to complain or ask for help or, in this case, even tell her friends that it was happening," Pamela said.

"Anyway," said Sam, now more cheerful as she held up the book, "Mrs. Whatley said she told you about Ruth Fenton and how she bullied Belinda and you asked if she had a photograph of Ruth.  She told me that the police officers came by and picked up all of Belinda's yearbooks that had Ruth's pictures in them. But they didn't take my yearbooks, and Mrs. Whatley suggested that you might like to borrow one so you could see what Ruth Fenton looks like."

"Oh, my!" cried Pamela, reaching forward and taking the yearbook in her hands.

"I've already looked at her," said Sam. "I've marked the page with the sticky note.  See!  There!" Pamela quickly flipped to the marked page and ran her finger down the list of photographs until she came to one labeled "Ruth Fenton."  Staring out from the page was the black and white face of a teen-aged girl. Her dark hair hung loosely around her chin. She wore a dark jumper and white blouse. Her eyes were large but dead as they stared morosely at the camera.

"Do you remember her, Sam?" asked Pamela.

"I vaguely do now," said Sam, narrowing her eyes. "I remember seeing her walking in the halls, I guess. But I never interacted with her. And, Dr. Barnes, Belinda never interacted with her—not that I can remember."

"Did Ruth have any friends?"

"I don't remember seeing her with other students— at least not with any great regularity," said Sam, "but, of course, I was focused on my own life and my friends and not on the activities of all the other students at school. I mean, Reardon High is a big school. When we were there, our graduating class was something like 500."

"How close were you and Belinda?"

"She was one of my best friends," said Sam. "As I told you, our mothers knew each other. They still do and are close friends. Maybe even more so because they're both widows; they both lost their husbands when they were fairly young and I think that helped them bond. Anyway, my mom always loved Belinda and Belinda's mom's always been great to me. Plus, our homes are close. Just a few blocks apart."

"It's strange though," added Pamela, "that Belinda never confided in you about this Ruth Fenton and the things she was doing to her."

"No," said Sam. "Not if you knew Belinda. She's just not a person who likes to dwell on negative things. She's always been...she always was one of the most positive people I've ever known. Like I told you.

Probably one of the reasons I liked her.   Jeeze, probably one of the reasons most everyone liked her!" She pulled a tissue from her pocket and wiped her eyes.

"If this girl was tormenting her," suggested Pamela, "then maybe she figured she'd just stop if she ignored her.  Or maybe she figured she could befriend her and get her to stop."

"The second one would be more like Belinda," said Sam.  "But if Ruth Fenton was mean to Belinda, you know, a mean girl, because she was jealous..."

"You think she was jealous?"

"Dr. Barnes," cried Sam, pointing at the photograph in the book on the professor's lap. "Look at her!  She's so mousy!  I barely remember her at all, probably because she faded into the woodwork.  Oh, I know that's horrible to say, but she could have been jealous of Belinda.   Belinda was beautiful and sweet and smart."

"It's strange," said Pamela staring intently at the face in the photograph, "you'd think it would be the other way around.   You'd think it would be the beautiful, popular girl like Belinda who would be bullying the mousy girl like this Ruth.  Instead, it's the mousy one who's the mean girl."

"I guess."

"Do you have any idea what things Ruth did to Belinda?"

"I didn't know anything about what she did at the time. But Mrs. Whatley told me on the phone just now about some of them.  She said once Ruth wrote a nasty note to one of the teachers and signed Belinda's name. Belinda got in a lot of trouble and really had a hard time convincing the teacher that she was innocent."

"Was she ever able to prove it was Ruth Fenton who did it?"

"Mrs. Whatley said Belinda knew it was Ruth," said Sam, "but she was just more concerned about clearing her own name than incriminating Ruth. That was just the way she was."

"And look where it got her," said Pamela pointedly, staring directly at Samantha. "Sometimes, you have to do more than just stand up for yourself. Sometimes, you have to point out the guilty person and let the chips fall where they may."

"Yes," said Sam. "That's why I brought you this yearbook, Dr. Barnes. That's why Belinda's mother wanted me to give it to you. We both know that you won't let Belinda's death be in vain. You'll do something about it. We hope having this photograph of Ruth Fenton will help you find out who killed Belinda—whether it's Ruth or not."

"I'm glad you brought it to me, Sam," said Pamela. "I don't know what I can do, but believe me, I'm going to try. I feel a certain responsibility to Belinda, even though I didn't know her personally. I was there when she was murdered. I feel like I've gotten to know her." She clutched the yearbook in her hands and stared intently at the photograph. "Now I need to get to know this young woman. Why would she do this to Belinda? Why did she hate her so much? Did the hatred she felt way back then that caused her to bully Belinda fester over the years and ultimately drive her to plot this horrible crime? And if so, how? How did she do it? She couldn't have just happened to be sitting in that seat in the audience on opening night that just happened to be placed so auspiciously right before the table where Belinda and her tea cup were located.  And how did she get the poison in the cup?  It must have been during the blackout?  How did she know about the blackout?  How did she know that Belinda would sit at that table after the blackout and drink from that cup?  There are so many questions and no answers—not yet."

"Not yet," said Samantha, sitting upright in the straight back chair.  "But, Dr. Barnes, I have faith that you'll find these answers."

"I hope you're right, Sam," said Pamela, shaking her head as she continued to stare at the photograph.  "I hope you're right.   And now that I have this photograph of Ruth Fenton, I believe I have a direction to go.  Some possible next steps to take."

"Then I'd better leave, Dr. Barnes," said Sam, rising, "so you can get going!"

## CHAPTER 26

Her enthusiasm was short lived. After the remaining student had finished seeking pre-test assistance, Pamela found herself left alone in her office to stare at the photograph of the forlorn-looking teenager. She suddenly felt sorry for the young woman in the picture. Surely this wasn't the face of a murderer. She was torn as she thought of her own daughter, Angela, and her childhood experiences with bullies. *Would any of them harbor hatred and resentment into adulthood and come back to make Angela's life miserable?* She couldn't imagine that people could hold grudges for so long. She couldn't. Ruth Fenton looked like a pitiful teenager, probably suffering through the same sort of emotional traumas that all other adolescents were going through.

Glancing at her wristwatch, she realized that it was now very late in the day. Her office hours were long over and no more students were lined up in the hallway to see her. She'd better gather her belongings and head home or at least call Rocky to let him know she was running late. He always appreciated updates on her arrival so he could plan the perfect dinner, bless his heart. It was the least she could do, and it was certainly preferable to going without a meal or—heaven forbid—cooking supper herself.

She grabbed her leather jacket from her coat tree and slipped it on. Then, slipping her purse over her shoulder, she carefully added the big red yearbook volume to the pile of papers and books she was carrying home to work on overnight. It made for a rather heavy load, but Pamela headed out into the now empty corridor, locked her office, and trudged down the stairwell into the main hallway of Blake Hall. She stopped by the Psychology Department's main office for a quick check of her mailbox. Sometimes, students left papers in her cubby hole or important documents arrived through inter-campus mail. The regular mail was delivered in the morning. As she reached into her box, she heard voices chattering in Jane Marie's small office around the corner.

"He's better," she heard the voice of Arliss sigh. "But now that he's better, he's moving around. Crawling. All over the place. I put him one place and when I turn around he's across the room. It's like a plot!" Arliss sounded depressed and exhausted. Just the other day, she'd been thrilled to learn that her baby had mastered crawling.

"He's a baby, Arliss!" chided Jane Marie, with a giggle. "Babies do crawl. It's how they learn, you know."

"Yes, dear," scolded Joan, "you'll just have to get used to his new mobility. You do want him to learn to walk, don't you?"

"Eventually," whined Arliss, "but I thought he'd just stay flat on his back for a while. Every day, he's doing something different. I can't rely on one behavior from one day to the next. I mean, with Bailey, our chimp, it's not like he's figured out how to open his cage."

"I hope you don't have Noah in a cage!" shrieked Jane Marie.

"Of course I don't," replied Arliss.

Pamela entered the secretary's alcove to discover her two pals seated in chairs across from Jane Marie's desk. They looked comfortably ensconced and were enjoying their chat. Jane Marie always seemed to like hearing—and giving—faculty gossip.

"Dr. Barnes!" cried Jane Marie, welcoming her. "Our new little mother seems to be suffering from parental exhaustion. She thought taking care of a baby would be no different from taking care of some of her lab rats."

"I did not!" scowled Arliss, scrunching herself over in her chair, crossing one leg over the other and pulling it tightly to her chest defensively. She yawned and sighed.

"Oh, come on," said Pamela. "Let's give her a break. We're all mothers and we know how exhausting infants are. Jane Marie, you have two! And they're still young. So you surely remember even better than Joan and I do!"

"Of course I do," replied Jane Marie. "I just can't help it. I mean that animal lab is always so neat and clean. Not a thing out of place. Arliss never seems at all frustrated by taking charge of all of that! It's just funny to see her so discombobulated by one infant!" She smiled warmly at Pamela and gestured at Arliss with another giggle.

"It's true," agreed Joan. She gave Arliss a nudge. "Where's that ol' animal lab director spirit? Anyone who can manage that place can surely control one tiny baby."

"Please!" cried Arliss, pulling her shoulders up around her ears. "I'm so tired! Why are you all teasing me so?"

"Because it's so much fun!" replied Joan lightly. "Look at yourself, Arliss! I mean, you're never a fashion plate. But I don't think you've combed your hair in a month!"

"Joan!" cried Pamela. "Give her a break. She needs our support, not our harassment."

"Pamela, you're a spoilsport," said Joan. "I need someone to tease; otherwise I'll go crazy with all this business with Belinda's murder."

"Do they have any new clues?" asked Jane Marie, looking from Joan to Pamela. She had ceased working on her document and now was leaning back in her desk chair, sipping from her coffee cup.

"Well, they wouldn't have gotten them from me," announced Joan, "although they keep sending officers back into my office to harass me with more questions. Unfortunately, they're always too young for me, and usually married." She said this last part with a definite twinkle in her eye.

"Joan," admonished Pamela. She shook her head. "Actually..." She looked around the room at her three friends. She set her belongings on the corner of Jane Marie's desk and held up the big, red yearbook. "Actually, I have what may turn out to be a clue. I'm not sure."

"What is it?" asked the secretary, stretching forward to see the contents of the volume. Joan and Arliss perked up.

"This is a high school yearbook. Belinda's high school yearbook."

"And the police suspect someone from her high school class?" asked Joan.

"Actually, I suspect someone from her high school," replied Pamela. "Of course, I've told Shoop—

Detective Shoop—about my suspicions.  I have reason to believe, after speaking with one of Belinda's close friends, who happens to be one of my thesis advisees…"

"Which one?" asked Joan.

"Samantha Landry," replied Pamela.

"I know her," said Jane Marie quickly.  She leaned her elbows on her desk.  "A very nice student."

"Yes," agreed Pamela.  "She's very upset about Belinda.  They've been friends for years.  Sam also is evidently very close to Belinda's mother.  Their mothers have been close since the two girls were children.  Sam told me she remembered Belinda's mother talking about some 'mean girls' who always pestered Belinda."

"Children can be such bullies," said Joan.  "Particularly girls.  They're often the worst."

"I hope Noah never gets bullied," added Arliss, peeking up over the top of her knees.

"You'll have to train him to be a feminist!" suggested Joan.

"Just like our boss!" added Pamela.

"Mitchell, a feminist?" cried Joan.  "Hardly!"

At the mention of his name, Department Head Mitchell Marks popped his head out of the door that led to his office.  "What are you hens chatting about out here?" he demanded cheerfully.  "Are you ladies distracting my secretary from her work?"

"Yes," said Joan.  "We were just discussing what a feminist you are, Mitchell!  You know, a champion of women's rights."

"Of course," replied Mitchell, deadpan.  "I love women."  He glanced at his animal laboratory director, sitting Buddha-like on the tiny wooden chair. "Arliss, did your new guinea pig die?"

"She's suffering from crawling baby syndrome, Mitchell," said Joan, a hand placed sympathetically on Arliss's shoulder.

"Indeed!" replied their boss. "My sympathies."

"Oh, Dr. Marks!" cried Jane Marie. "Dr. Barnes has a new clue in the murder of that young woman who was poisoned during the play."

"Do tell," said Mitchell, looking quizzically at Pamela across the small alcove.

"I was just telling them, Mitchell," she said, "that I've determined that Belinda Purvis was evidently bullied a lot when she was younger by a young woman named Ruth Fenton. I've even got a copy of the Reardon High School yearbook during the time when Belinda and this Ruth were students there. I think there's a possibility that Ruth Fenton may have been the person who poisoned her."

"So show us her photo, Pamela!" exclaimed Joan. "Don't just stand there clutching that book!"

Pamela sighed and flipped open the book to the bookmarked page. She ran her finger down to Ruth Fenton's photograph and turned the yearbook around and displayed it for everyone to see.

"That's the killer?" asked Arliss, staring intently at the picture Pamela was holding up.

"I don't know for sure," she began. "But..."

"Eek," said Joan, "she's mousy. Isn't she? If she bullied Belinda it was probably out of jealousy." That was her pronouncement and she ended it with a dramatic gesture.

"I agree," said Jane Marie, pulling the yearbook closer to her. Pamela willingly moved around the room holding the book aloft so all four people could get a good view of Ruth Fenton. "She's not very attractive. Of course, that was many years ago. She could look a lot different now."

"True," said Mitchell as Pamela stood at attention while he perused the interior page of the Reardon High School yearbook. "Knowing you women, she's probably a blue-eyed blonde! Probably with fake breasts."

"This photograph wasn't taken that many years ago," said Pamela, turning the book so she could see the picture again. "Belinda was only 26. So I'm assuming this Ruth Fenton was—is about the same age. I'm trying to imagine what she might look like. I have reason to believe she was in the audience the night of the play, seated close to the table, and may have placed the poison in Belinda's cup during the blackout."

"You mean a front row seat near the table?" asked Joan.

"Yes," said Pamela. "Do you remember her there?"

"Why do you think she was there?" asked Jane Marie.

"Actually, by a process of elimination. Rocky and I were in seats C6 and C7 and he remembers an elderly couple in C8 and C9. The seat on the end of the row which was right in front of the table was C10 and that's where we think this Ruth Fenton might have been seated. Of course, the Coffee Factory doesn't have a record of who purchased the ticket, but they know it wasn't a season ticket holder. It must have been someone who bought the ticket in advance or at the door."

"Joan," said Arliss, turning to her friend, "you were seated there. Could you see anyone in the audience?"

"It was possible," replied Joan, "but really the audience was a sea of faces. I was so totally focused on my part that I didn't really notice who was in the audience or where. I only vaguely remember seeing Pamela and Rocky there. I couldn't even tell you now where they were seated."

"That's too bad," noted Mitchell Marks, standing casually against the doorjamb to his office. "Joan, you could solve this mystery and then we'd have two detectives in our department instead of one!" He smiled amiably at Pamela.

"Let me see that photograph, Pamela," said Joan, as if in response to Mitchell's prod. She grabbed the yearbook from Pamela's hands and brought the photograph of Ruth Fenton close to her eyes, squinting intently at the teen's picture. "Hmm, she does look a little familiar. I can't think where I've seen this person—or maybe an older version of this person. Certainly, not with this horrible hairdo! But the face does look familiar."

"I'm thinking that you may not be the only person who might recognize her," said Pamela.

"Really?" asked Jane Marie, her eyes lit with excitement. "Who else?"

"Are any of you willing to take a little trip with me?" she asked.

"Sorry, Pamela," replied Mitchell, starting to return to his office. "Got a department heads' meeting at five. Otherwise...you ladies go ahead."

"Me?" asked Jane Marie. "It's only four thirty."

"I'll cover for you, Jane Marie," replied the man. "After all, I am a feminist. Secretarial duties are not beneath me. The four of you go track down whatever Pamela wants you to track down."

With a certain amount of glee, the four women gathered their things and headed out of the building and into the parking lot. A little caravan of cars drove valiantly to keep up with Pamela's Civic as it careened through the winding campus streets and into the nearby downtown area.

**CHAPTER 27**

They were all in a booth at the back of the Coffee Factory.  The yearbook, open to Ruth Fenton's photograph, held the place of honor in the center of the wooden table, as the four women, mugs of alternative coffee drinks in hand, bent over it, their heads almost touching as they squinted at the woman's face.  Like the last time they were here, the Coffee Factory was almost empty.  There were several men in suits seated at a table near the front window. The waitress who had seated them and brought them their drinks was now languishing at the front counter reading a gossip magazine.

"I wish you could remember where you saw her," said Pamela to Joan, with a sigh.  She slurped up the last of her apple cinnamon coffee whip, a little frothy cream remaining on her upper lip.

"I'm racking my brain, Pamela," replied Joan, still sipping her own drink neatly.  The cranberry-blueberry mixture did not even stain her teeth.  "Whoever this person is, she'd be eight years older now.  She's probably changed a lot and looks much different."

"She was probably one of your students, Dr. Bentley," suggested Jane Marie from across the table. Like Joan, Pamela noticed, Jane Marie was a neat drinker.  You'd think all the cherries that went into the cherry smash coffee she was drinking would surely come to rest somewhere on her mouth, but they didn't. Pamela didn't need to look at herself in her compact mirror to guess what she probably looked like.

"And she's female," added Arliss, slouched back in the corner of the booth, her mug of mint julep coffee clenched against her jaw. The green mixture was dribbling precariously from the corner of her mouth. Arliss smiled at Joan sweetly. "You never remember any of your female students."

"That's not true!" cried Joan, picking up the small, tan paper napkin that had been resting under her mug and giving her mouth a totally unnecessary wipe. "I have a good memory for faces—of both sexes."

"If Belinda took classes in our department," said Jane Marie, "then it's surely possible that Ruth Fenton did too. Think hard, Dr. Bentley."

"Maybe if you went back and checked your grade books for the last few years," suggested Pamela, following Joan's lead and wiping her own mouth with the available small paper napkin. Hers came away with a large dollop of whipped cream that she hadn't realized was there.

"She wasn't a student!" declared Joan, setting down her drink emphatically.

At that moment, Silvus Barge appeared from the kitchen and wandered over to the women in the booth. "Ladies!" he said warmly. "We're so delighted to have you back with us again."

"We brought along our departmental secretary," said Pamela.

"Administrative assistant," corrected Jane Marie sweetly, holding up her hand in greeting.

"Jane Marie Mira, this is Silvus Barge, owner of the Coffee Factory."

Barge took her hand and gave it a perfunctory kiss. "Delighted," he said with a romantic sweep of his other hand.  Jane Marie's eyes lit up.

"Ooo!" she giggled.  "We'll have to come here more often."

"Please do," replied Barge.  "Are you ladies out sleuthing again?"

"Actually," said Pamela, taking the yearbook and turning it around so Barge could see the photograph of Ruth Fenton straight up, "we're trying to locate this young woman, Silvus.  This is her yearbook photo from eight years ago.  She and Belinda Purvis were apparently at odds during their high school days and Belinda's mother thinks this Ruth may still bear a grudge against her daughter."

"Hmm," he said as he stared at the picture.  Pamela held up the book so the large man could get a better view of the suspect.  "I can't say that I've seen her or know her.  Of course, I don't really know any of Belinda's friends.  It's not as if she brought any of them to rehearsals or down here.  Did she, Joan?"

"No," said Joan.  "The only person who ever came to rehearsals with Belinda was her husband, and he only came to pick her up afterwards.  He never stayed and watched us."

"Nor did he ever come down here after rehearsals when you cast members would sometimes sit here late at night and unwind or go over your lines," added Barge.  He rubbed his large, fleshy palms together as he continued to stare at the photograph.  "I don't know.  Maybe she looks a little familiar.  Maybe Dottie knows who she is."

"Yes," said Pamela, pulling the book back and setting it in the middle of the table.  "Is she here?

Could you ask her to come out, Silvus, and take a look at this photo?"

"I certainly can," he said and immediately headed off into the kitchen.

"This is all probably a real long shot, Pamela," said Arliss, squeezing her arms around her legs in the far corner of the booth. "Some girl the dead girl knew in high school? How likely is it that she did this? Or that, if she did, no one recognized her?"

"She certainly doesn't seem very memorable," said Jane Marie, peering again at the tiny picture in the book. "She's so nondescript. Only those eyes. They really are—I don't know what—lifeless."

"Yes," agreed Pamela. "She seems sad. Not a very good way to pose for your yearbook picture."

"Maybe so," agreed Joan. "But I just can't help thinking that I've seen her somewhere. I just can't figure out where."

Silvus Barge returned, followed by Dottie Ibberly. The little business manager had to take two steps for every one of Barge's just to keep up with the big man's strides. They arrived at the booth.

"Dottie," said Silvus. "These ladies have a photograph they'd like to show you." He gestured for the elderly woman to move to the edge of table. Pamela picked up the yearbook and held it up in front of Dottie Ibberly. She pointed to Ruth Fenton's photograph.

"This girl," said Pamela. "Have you ever seen her, Dottie? Of course, this photograph was taken eight years ago, so she'd be older now."

"Hmmm," said Dottie, holding her wire frame glasses tightly in both hands as she adjusted them, evidently for a clearer view. "Hmmm. She does look a little familiar.  Now who does she look like?"  All four women in the booth stared at the little woman, glaring at the photograph.  Silvus Barge focused his attention on the entire group.

"Maybe a customer?" asked Silvus.  Dottie continued to stare and say nothing.  Silvus was becoming noticeably agitated.  "Someone who came in to buy a ticket for the show?"

"No," said Dottie finally.  "No, I don't think so.  She looks...she looks....you know, she looks a lot like Rachel Williams!"

"Who's that?" asked the entire group at once.

"Yes," said Dottie, ignoring their questions as she continued to stare at the photograph.  "I do believe that that *is* Rachel.  Of course, she's a blonde now, but I recognize her face.  And her eyes.  So strange.  She's not a very cheerful girl.  You can see that from her picture.  Yes, the more I look at it, the more I'm sure it's Rachel."

"Dottie!" cried Silvus, attempting to get the woman's attention away from the photograph.  "Who is this person?"

"Oh," said Dottie, looking up and around the table.  "Rachel is one of our waitresses.  She's on the day staff.  Of course, I haven't seen her in a while because Silvus has had to cut back since the...since Belinda's death."

"So, the person in this photo works here?" asked Pamela.

"Yes," said Dottie.  "That's what I'm saying.  I believe this is a photograph of Rachel Williams and she works here."

"I thought you said her name is Ruth Fenton," said Arliss, flinging her feet to the ground and leaning over the table.

"I don't know what she told you," replied Dottie, "but she told us her name is Rachel Williams and that's how I have her listed and that's how I submit her tax forms to the government."

"How long has she worked here?" asked Pamela.

"Not long," replied Dottie. "She started a few months ago. She's very good. Efficient. Quiet, but efficient. I don't think she makes very good tips, because she's not terribly chatty with the customers, but she's responsible and I've had no complaints about her work."

"My goodness!" cried Joan. "Could it be? I do think I remember her waiting on the cast one time."

"Did she buy a ticket for the production?" asked Pamela.

"I don't know," said Dottie. "As I told you the other day, I only keep records of ticket sales to season ticket holders and reservations made in advance. She could have bought a ticket and paid cash. I mean, she has access to the cash register and the tickets. As long as she paid for the ticket, if she bought one and put money in the cash register for it, we wouldn't mind."

"What about observing rehearsals?" asked Pamela.

"She could have watched rehearsals," replied Dottie. "Any of our waiters and waitresses could. In fact, as I mentioned, they all needed to be aware of the seating arrangement in the theater so they could answer customer questions. Any of them could go upstairs while a rehearsal was in progress and watch it. I'm sure some of them did just that."

"She could have seen our scene," cried Joan.

"She could have known just where that table was and when Belinda would sit there and when she would drink from that cup," added Pamela.

"And when the blackout would occur," said Joan, "which would give her the opportunity to put the poison in Belinda's cup."

"I told you all this the other day when we were up there in the theater looking around," whined Arliss. "Why don't you listen to me? I said that someone sitting in that one seat could just reach over and touch the actress at the table."

"You did, indeed," said Pamela, nodding.

"And Dottie," added Silvus, "you would have no idea about this Rachel and her background?"

"No more than you, Silvus," shot back Dottie. "I'm the business manager. I'm in the back room most of the day. You're the one who's out here in the restaurant all the time. I'm surprised you didn't recognize her from this photograph. And—if any of the waitresses decided to sneak up to the theater and watch rehearsals, I'd think it would be you who would notice. Didn't you notice her?"

"I regret to say," said Silvus Barge sadly, "that I don't even know who this woman is."

"Well," said Dottie, "you'll find out soon."

"Why is that?" asked Pamela, excited.

"Because I just called her in to substitute for one of our night waitresses who called in sick. She should be here in about twenty minutes."

## CHAPTER 28

Pamela had made several strategic phone calls and the group had developed a makeshift plan for how to handle the arrival of Ruth Fenton/Rachel Williams. Now all they had to do was wait and see what happened when the young woman appeared for her shift. They didn't have to wait long, because, as Dottie Ibberly had predicted, the waitress was right on time. Pamela was the first to notice her enter through the restaurant's main door, the bell tinkling to announce her arrival—not that any of them needed any warning.

Pamela had already placed the red yearbook on the bench seat next to her. The women had all re-ordered their original coffee drinks and were enjoying the refills and chatting amiably when Pamela gave them the agreed upon signal that Rachel Williams had entered the premises. The young waitress walked up to the front counter and began chatting softly with the waitress on duty. Soon, the two women traded places, the first waitress removing her apron and depositing it somewhere under the counter. She marked a form behind the counter and then grabbed a jacket and a purse and waved good-bye to her replacement. Rachel removed her outer garments, signed in, and then looked up at the customers in the restaurant. She then grabbed a coffee pot from a nearby stand and headed over to the two men by the window who waved her away when she attempted to refill their cups.

"Here she comes," said Pamela under her breath, as she was situated so she could see the waitress's approach.

"Can I get you ladies anything else?" Rachel asked softly. At first glance, the waitress didn't resemble Ruth Fenton. Her hair was lighter and styled neatly in a pageboy. Her eyes were lighter too, not the brown they appeared to be in the photograph.

"Oh," said Pamela, "we all had specialty drinks." All four of them held up their mugs, continuing to sip noisily on their drinks, and smiled.

"Would any of you like refills on those?" asked the waitress. She looked around. Her round face and the dead glaze of her eyes were identical to those of the girl in the picture. Pamela realized that she was staring at Ruth Fenton, former mean girl, and probable killer of Belinda Purvis.

"These are our seconds," replied Pamela. "Thanks." The woman started to turn away when Pamela stopped her. "Oh, Miss..." The young woman turned and returned to the table where all four women continued to smile at her. "Oh, I was just wondering," continued Pamela, " if you knew the young woman who was killed recently in that show that was performed upstairs here?"

"Uh..." stammered Ruth Fenton, alias Rachel Williams, for as Pamela looked at her close up, she was now thoroughly convinced that this was indeed the same person whose photograph was in Belinda Purvis's yearbook. The yearbook she held beside her on the bench.

"You know," said Pamela encouragingly, "it's been all over the news. Surely you know about it since you work here."

"I...uh, don't pay that much attention..." mumbled the waitress, turning to go.

"You don't remember me?" asked Joan. "I played Lady Bracknell, the mother of the actress who was murdered. I was down here frequently with the cast. We often came here to drink and practice our lines."

"I don't usually work this shift," replied Ruth/Rachel weakly. She again quickly turned to leave.

"Wait a minute!" cried Pamela, stopping the young woman in her tracks. "Wait a minute. You know, I think I know you." She grabbed the woman's wrist tightly.

"I...uh...don't know you," said Ruth/Rachel, trying to twist out of Pamela's tight hold on her arm.

"Oh?" said Pamela. "Aren't you Ruth Fenton?" The woman's face turned beet red. She froze; her attempts to move ended. She stared at Pamela, her dead expression turning to one of smoldering hatred. "Aren't you one of Belinda's high school friends? You remember? Belinda Purvis, born Belinda Whatley?" The waitress remained silent.

"Of course!" cried Joan, joining in the game. "I remember Belinda talking about you! Ruth Fenton. She told us all about you. She said you used to torment her when the two of you were in school together."

"Why would you do that?" asked Jane Marie, emboldened evidently by Pamela's firm grip on the young woman's wrist.

"Yeh," added Arliss. "It's not nice to be mean to little kids, you know." She sneered at the waitress, who shook her head and let her eyes jump back and forth from one woman to another.

"Who are you people?" cried Ruth/Rachel, struggling to get her hand free. She finally extricated herself from the grip and stood belligerent in front of the booth. "Who are you? Why are you attacking me? I don't know what you're talking about."

Pamela removed the yearbook beside her and flipped it open to the page where Ruth Fenton's photograph was posted. She held it up before the woman.

"This is you, isn't it?" she demanded. "This is you, Ruth Fenton. Back when you were in school. Back when you were a mean girl and for reasons unknown, took it upon yourself to taunt Belinda Purvis. A girl who never did anything to you. Nothing! Yet, you went out of your way to play pranks on her and make her life miserable. Everyone thought you'd moved on. Even Belinda. She was fine with that. She had no desire for retribution. No desire to get back at you. She never did. She was a sweet young woman, at least according to her mother and her best friend Samantha Landry. And now, after all these years, for some reason, you come back to finish her off! It wasn't enough just to tease her. You had to kill her. Why? What had this woman ever done to you that you concocted this immensely convoluted scheme to poison her during opening night of her debut performance?"

"Yes," added Joan, "we all want to know! Why did you do this?"

"We know you did it, Ruth," said Pamela, glaring at her. "We know about how you purchased a ticket in advance, how all the wait staff here at the Coffee Factory are expected to be knowledgeable about the seating arrangement in the theater, about how they can all slip upstairs and watch rehearsals when they're not busy. I'm guessing you were up there quite a bit and spent a lot of time watching where Belinda sat. I just bet you noticed that she sat at that little table and drank tea from a cup and that the table was easily reachable by anyone seated in C10. It wouldn't have been at all difficult for you to buy seat C10 for opening night. No one had to know. So during the blackout right before Belinda's scene, you just reached over and poured arsenic into her cup and then sat back and waited for her to drink it. Then you reacted with shock right along with the entire audience when she collapsed, and left when the rest of the audience left. It was incredibly easy. Easy. We can explain how you did it, Ruth, but what we can't explain is why you did it. Why did you hate Belinda so much and for so long that you felt you had to kill her?" Ruth remained standing, frozen, her body shaking. She looked like she might speak but no words escaped her mouth.

"Because she had everything!" yelled Ruth Fenton finally, her whole body heaving with sobs as she clutched her face in her hands. "She had everything. She always had everything—and I had nothing. I loved it when she was drinking the poison and then she couldn't speak. She made those horrible sounds. It was the best moment in my life. For once—just once––things weren't right for her, and there was nothing she could do about it. It was the best moment in my life!"

Then, all of a sudden, she bolted for the kitchen exit. However, before she could make it through the curtains, she was stopped by two police officers barring her way. Right behind them, Detective Shoop entered.

"Arrest this woman," he said to the officers, who immediately clasped handcuffs on Ruth Fenton and took her away through the back entrance, struggling all the way. The men seated at the table near the front rose in shock, but returned to their chairs once the officers had led the suspect out. Throughout the entire scene, Ruth Fenton glowered back at Pamela, but said nothing.

Once they had gone, Shoop wandered over to Pamela and her three friends at the booth.

"I must thank you, Dr. Barnes," said Shoop, "for doing my job for me—again. I assume you got all of that on your little audio recorder?"

"Right here," replied Pamela, pulling the small device from her skirt pocket. "Never go anywhere without one."

"I have a feeling the DA will want to hear all of that," he said. "Probably will want to use it in the trial."

"That was amazing!" cried Jane Marie, flush with excitement. "I can't believe I just witnessed the arrest of a murder suspect."

"Motherhood pales in comparison!" added Arliss. "Give me a nice calm afternoon of chasing after a toddler."

"And most important of all," declared Joan dramatically, "now with Belinda's murder solved, we can finally get the show going again." Silvus Barge and Dottie Ibberly had entered from the kitchen. They crowded around the booth listening to Shoop and Pamela discuss the capture of the killer.

"I can't believe that Rachel actually poisoned that poor girl!" cried Dottie. "She didn't seem like she could hurt a flea."

"She certainly didn't look very intimidating," said Barge in agreement. "I guess, Dottie, we'll have to be a lot more careful about who we hire."

"You're right, Silvus," said the little grey-haired woman, "it's just not enough that they're punctual."

Everyone chuckled at that.

"So, Shoop," said Pamela, "what happens next? I mean, what will happen to Ruth Fenton now?"

"She'll be arraigned," he said. "There will be a bail hearing although I doubt that she'll get out on bail."

"Too much of a flight risk?" asked Pamela.

"Yes," said Shoop.

"We don't even know if she has family in Reardon," suggested Joan.

"We don't" agreed Pamela. "She was so wrapped up in Belinda and what she had. For all we know, she might have a very wonderful family who will be devastated by this."

"Whatever," added Shoop, flicking his perennial hanky across his nose with a dramatic toss, "the bunch of you are done with this case." He pointed his finger at Pamela and then at each of the women at the booth. "Enjoy your drinks, ladies!" With that, he headed out the front door. The two men by the window followed him out with their eyes and then glanced back and Pamela and her friends.

"Wow!" said Arliss when the foursome was finally all alone. "That was something!"

"The most exciting thing I've experienced in ages!" agreed Jane Marie.

"I'm certainly glad that woman didn't pull a gun from her purse and shoot us all!" said Joan.

"Unlikely," said Pamela.

"Why do you say that, Pamela?" asked Arliss.

"From all your crime-solving experience?" asked Jane Marie.

"No," replied Pamela.  "It's just that she's a poisoner and poisoning is not a very aggressive method of murder.  It's sort of a wimpy way, if you think about it.  No confrontation.  She never confronted Belinda directly.  She always tormented her from afar.  I'm not sure that Belinda even knew all the times that Ruth Fenton played pranks on her.  Probably there were a lot of 'accidents' that happened that might have been caused by Ruth that Belinda never was aware of."

"Something tells me, Pamela," said Joan, "that there will be one big confrontation tonight when you tell your overprotective mate about this little episode."

"Oh, Joan!" moaned Pamela, head in her hands. "Don't remind me!"  They all laughed.

## CHAPTER 29

Joan was right.  Pamela was dreading confronting Rocky with the news of the capture of Ruth Fenton alias Rachel Williams even more than she had dreaded confronting the killer at the Coffee Factory.  And why should she?  She was surrounded by her friends and a troupe of police as back-up when she faced the young killer.  She had to face Rocky alone.

She steered her little Civic into her garage.  It was past her usual arrival time and she hadn't called Rocky to let him know she'd be late.  There had been so much excitement and upheaval when they had discovered that Ruth/Rachel would be arriving at the Coffee Factory soon.  She just didn't have time to call.  Actually she just didn't think about calling.  Now she was regretting her actions.  As soon as the loud garage door mechanism came to a stop, Rocky appeared at their kitchen door, apron on, a mixing bowl tucked in one arm and a big wooden spoon clutched in the other hand.  He looked annoyed.  At least, she hoped that was his annoyed look and not something worse.

"Hi!" she called cheerily as she ducked out of the driver's side and reached across the gear shift for her purse and papers.  "I hope I didn't keep you waiting too long."  She gave him her sweetest and most sheepish look and headed towards the door.  Rocky remained speechless but opened the door, allowing her to enter. "Wow! What a day! You'll never believe!"

"I'm sure," he mumbled in a monotone and snapped the door shut behind her.

"Yum!" she chirped. "It sure smells good in here! What are you cooking?"

"You mean what *did* I cook?" he corrected. "I ate an hour ago. There are leftovers in the fridge. I'm just whipping up a batch of muffins for your lunches for next week."

"Oh!" she replied. "Nice! Sorry, I'm late. I didn't realize it was…"

"After seven," he said, glancing at his watch. "Was there some sort of…emergency?"

"Actually," she began, setting her belongings on the dining room table, "they caught the killer of that woman who was poisoned!"

"Great!" he replied blandly. "Why does that make you so late?"

"Well," she said, cringing, "I was sort of part of the capture."

"What?"

"Joan and Arliss and Jane Marie were too!" she added, quickly. "I mean, I wasn't alone. And Shoop and several officers were there too!" She smiled giddily at him as she backed into the kitchen and attempted to open the refrigerator door while continuing to maintain her happy face. "That's why I didn't have time to call you. Everything just happened so fast, Rocky! Please understand." She leaned against the refrigerator with the plate of leftovers clutched to her chest.

"You realize that I'm mad because I was worried, don't you?" he asked, moving closer to her, his nose almost touching hers over the top of the covered plate.

"I know," she whimpered. "I'm really sorry. I know how worried you must have been. But everything worked out fine. It really did!" She stood up taller and gave him a very bright smile, peeking sideways at the plate of food. "This really smells good. I can hardly wait to eat it."

"Go! Go!" he said finally with frustration, motioning for her to sit at the dining table. She sped to the table and ripped the top off the plate. He handed her a fork from the kitchen drawer and she began eating, continuing to talk between mouthfuls.

"Oh, Rocky!" she mumbled. "You should have been there! It was amazing! This woman is a waitress at the Coffee Factory. Four of us—Arliss, Jane Marie, and, of course, Joan, were all there. And when we started to ask her about Belinda, you could just see in her eyes that she realized that she'd been discovered!"

"And just how did you accomplish that, Sherlock?" he asked, setting down a glass of red wine next to her place and joining her on the other side of the table.

"Where's Candide?" she asked, looking around for her little buddy.

"It's probably even too late for him," suggested her husband.

"But there's food," she declared. "Candide! Candide!" After a few seconds, a little fuzzy head appeared at the bedroom door. "Mommy's home!" she called to the dog, who suddenly energized, no doubt more because of the availability of food rather than the late return of his mistress. "Here's a nibble for you." She pulled off a piece of the little meat tartlet that Rocky had obviously spent hours slaving over and handed it to her pet.

"It's wasted on him," noted Rocky.

"You have two very appreciative customers tonight, Mr. Barnes," she said, her eyes twinkling.

"I suppose if I even attempt to scold you or express my worry and concern, I'll never hear the end of it," he added.   He rubbed his chin with his hand and she reached over and gently touched his stubble-covered cheek.

"I love your worry and concern," she said, "as long as it's for me."

"Who else? So, this woman, this waitress, she was the one who killed the actress?" he asked.

"Yep," replied Pamela.  "It's a long story, but suffice it to say that one of my thesis advisees led me to Belinda's mother who talked about a mean girl from Belinda's past who was always playing pranks on her. When we started to realize that the person who was sitting in C10..."

"The seat in the audience?"

She quickly explained how they had figured out who Ruth Fenton was and laid their trap for her.  As usual, Rocky was worried for his wife's welfare and expressed his concern about their plan.

"She might have had a gun or a knife in her pocket."

"I doubt it, Rocky," replied Pamela, having finished the tiny pie and leaning her forehead against her mate's. "I think she chose poison as her preferred means of murder because she's just not aggressive enough to do anything directly.  In fact, according to Belinda's mother, all of her pranks were that way too–

–she never really confronted Belinda. It was really very sad. More sad than scary."

"Okay, okay," he said, nuzzling his wife warmly. "I guess I'll never change you. Not that I want to—at least not the real you. I'd just like to make you a little less daring."

"Believe me, there was no daring involved today. It was quite anti-climactic."

"Good. Now, just let me clean up and we can go to bed."

"Bed?" she cried. "It's only eight o'clock! I'm not at all sleepy!"

"I can't win!" he declared. "It's either too late or too early! And," he paused. "I didn't say we had to sleep," he finished suggestively.

"Oh," she said and smiled, eyelashes fluttering, "you didn't say anything about the not sleeping part."

"I suppose that now that the case has been solved, they'll try to stage that play again," he scowled.

"Oh, yes!" she said enthusiastically. "They've already scheduled rehearsals. The director found a new actress to replace Belinda Purvis. With any luck, it should just take them a few weeks to get it going."

"Good, I guess."

"They were really anxious to restage it. Joan even asked me to audition for the Gwendolyn role. Can you imagine?"

"You? Acting in a play?" He practically sputtered with laughter.

"Is it such a strange idea?" she asked defensively. "I bet I could do it. I mean, I'm a teacher. I stand up in front of students and talk every day. It's not like I'm afraid of speaking in public."

"Yeah," he said, "but that's a lot different from pretending you're some fancy society belle. And you'd have to memorize lines! Ick!" He continued to laugh.

"Rocky!" she cried. "What's the matter with you? I bet I would make a good Gwendolyn!"

"Well, thank God we don't have to find out! You said they've already recast the role."

"They have, but maybe I'll do a play there in the future," she said, her chin stuck out defiantly.

"Not if I have anything to say about it!" he cried, still laughing heartily.

"What?" she cried. "You can't stop me!"

"I know that!" he exclaimed. "I've never been able to stop you from doing anything you've ever put your mind to."

"Then, why do you think you could prevent me from trying out for a production at the Reardon Little Theater?"

"I don't know," he replied, the laughter subsiding. "I guess it's just that I don't see sleuthing and acting as going together well."

"Probably not," she agreed with a sigh. "But it might be fun."

"Humph," he snorted. "You're just thinking about those stage kisses with some young galoot," he pouted.

"Oh, Rocky," she whispered, "I have no interest in kissing anyone but you." She nibbled his ear seductively. "Didn't you say something earlier about wanting to go to bed?"

"I did," he replied, rising and grabbing her hand and leading her off to their bedroom. Candide awoke from his position at Pamela's feet and pranced behind them. "Not tonight, buddy!" Rocky shut the door in the face of the little dog who gave a short whimper and returned to his other sleeping spot under the table.

## CHAPTER 30

"Oh, wow!" said Arliss, in a muffled whisper to Pamela, seated to her left in the front row of the Reardon Little Theater. They were in seats C6 and C7——the very ones where Pamela and Rocky had sat during the original and fateful production of 'The Importance of Being Earnest.' "This is close. I can reach my foot out and touch that little table." She did just that, stretching her long leg forward and scooting down in the velvet cushion of the seat.

"Arliss!" cried Pamela in a hushed whisper. She glanced around at the other audience members to see if they were offended by her pal's gaffe. "You're not supposed to do that. Just because you can touch the scenery in theater-in-the-round doesn't mean you should." Arliss pulled her leg back discreetly and sat up, shaking off the scolding. "I can't help it, Pam. I'm really antsy. It's hard to just sit here."

"I'd think you'd be thrilled to just be able to relax for a while, knowing Bob's home taking care of Noah." Pamela placed her hand on Arliss's arm which was clutching the side of the theater seat, as she looked around the place.

"It certainly looks a lot different with all the lights and fancy props," she said. "Not at all like it did the day we all came up here to search for clues. It seemed very drab then."

"I know what you mean," agreed Pamela, leaning sideways to her friend and chatting close to her ear. "This is really exciting, isn't it? I mean, even more so because of all the horrible events of the first performance."

"Let's just hope nothing like that occurs again," said Arliss, turning and nodding at her friend. "Do you think all these people are expecting something bad to happen?"

"I hope not," said Pamela emphatically. "Now that Ruth Fenton is safely locked up, she won't be a threat to anyone anymore."

"Can you believe what they found at her apartment?" asked Arliss, shaking her head. Pamela had followed the aftermath of the Belinda Purvis murder as it had played out in the news over the last few weeks. She knew that Arliss was referring to the report that the police had discovered the rotting corpses of several small dogs and other animals in a shed behind the rental house where Ruth Fenton lived. The police surmised that she had used these poor creatures to test out appropriate doses of arsenic so that she would be able to deliver a massively lethal amount in Belinda's cup on stage with minimal effort.

"It's horrible, I know," agreed Pamela, not wanting to even mention the disgusting murderer and her strange behavior in the very place where she had accomplished her deadly purpose. "But, I think—I hope they're all thinking positively just like us. I'm just expecting a wonderful show. I know at least the first scene is superb. You'll love it! And Joan! Wait until you see her! Arliss, you'll never believe how good she is."

"Oh, I can believe she's good," said Arliss. "Joan is nothing if not dramatic." She gave Pamela a contained eye roll. Both women were speaking softly so as not to disturb the other people sitting on either side of them and behind. "You're sure your husband doesn't mind giving me his seat?"

"Are you kidding?" she laughed softly. "He said he felt like he was on stage. He would have been happy to leave early—even if there hadn't been a murder during the performance."

"I can understand his feeling about this stage," said Arliss, pulling her legs in tightly under her seat. "It's like those people over across the way are all staring at me."

"Maybe they are," said Pamela. "But they probably feel the same about you. But don't worry. Once the show starts, you'll forget all about them and just concentrate on the play."

"People sure do get all dressed up for these things," said Arliss, looking around. Pamela realized that Arliss was used to wearing her slacks and sneakers everywhere. It had probably taken some mighty clever arguments on Bob's part to get her to actually put on dress pants and a pair of ballet flats. "Look at that woman across the way on the aisle; she's wearing a hat. Surely, you shouldn't wear hats here. The people behind you won't be able to see." Pamela strained to see where Arliss was indicating and she was right. There was a tiny woman seated in the second row in what Pamela now realized was section A, wearing a small hat. It was hardly grounds for concern as the woman was so short and the hat so flat that she doubted the person behind her would have any difficulty seeing over her.

"I guess this is a social event for many people," suggested Pamela. "You know, an opportunity to wear one's finery." She smiled at Arliss, and looked down at her own dress which was indeed one of the nicer outfits she possessed. Unfortunately, her efforts appeared lost on Arliss who never seemed the slightest bit interested in clothes, jewelry, or make-up. Pamela had a normal female concern for such issues—not an obsessive concern—but a normal one.

"Why?" asked Arliss with a shrug. "Who cares what people in the audience wear? I'd think they'd be more interested in what the characters in the play wear."

"Yes," agreed Pamela. "And the costumes are wonderful! Wait until you see them! Oh, Arliss, I'm so glad you were able to come tonight. This will be much more fun with you than with Rocky. He was such a spoilsport."

"To get away from child care for just a few hours," Arliss proclaimed in her soft voice, "I'd volunteer to sweep up poop after a herd of elephants in a touring circus. You can't imagine the stench of Noah's diapers when…"

"Oh, Arliss," said Pamela, "you love that baby, you know you do!" She realized that Arliss, like all mothers, needed an opportunity to get away from motherhood from time to time. After all, motherhood was a twenty-four hour a day job. It wasn't like your regular job where you could go home when the clock struck five—or six, or even seven. She'd loved taking care of Angela when her daughter was little, but she also knew how much she appreciated a few hours of freedom every now and then.

Arliss leaned back and rested her head of curly black hair against the top of the seat. "Oh, Pam! It just feels so good to be an adult for a while!" She sighed.

"I know," said Pamela. "And there's nothing more adult than Edwardian comedy! So prepare yourself."

A distant beeping noise distracted Pamela. Was that part of the show? Arliss gasped and suddenly reached into her back pants' pocket and drew out her ringing cell phone.

"It's Bob," she said. "Oh, no! I hope Noah's not worse!" She pushed a button and held the device close to her ear. "Yes. Yes. No. Okay." Pamela listened to the one-sided conversation attempting to determine what, if anything was wrong. There was a long pause as Arliss listened intently. Slowly, her face changed from dread to beaming.

"Yes! Noah, I'm your mommy!" She clasped the phone to her chest and whispered to Pamela. "He said 'Mommy'! Bob called to have him tell me!" She listened again to the phone and obviously was now speaking to Bob. After a few more joyous reactions and another quick comment to her son, Arliss closed her phone and glowed with delight.

"I guess you don't need to go home," said Pamela.

"He said 'Mommy'!" she repeated. Pamela patted her hand.

"I know, dear," she said. "Probably the best sounds in the world! Ooops! The house lights are dimming. We'll have to be quiet. You'd better put your phone on silent."

Arliss obeyed and sat up straight, just as darkness began to spread over the little theater.

"You didn't bring your audio recorder, did you?" she asked Pamela with a nudge.

"Not this time," replied Pamela. "I intend to ignore any unusual sounds and just enjoy myself!"

"Me too!" said Arliss. They smiled at each other as their faces faded away, replaced by the fictional world in the middle of the little theater-in-the-round.

**Rocky's Recipes**

*Cheesy Egg and Ham Breakfast Muffins*

6 eggs
chopped ham
shredded cheddar cheese
chopped red bell pepper
1 tsp. Italian seasoning
salt and pepper to taste

Grease a six-tin muffin pan.  Stir eggs together thoroughly and add seasoning.  Place mounds of ham, cheese, and bell pepper in the bottoms of each muffin tin.   Bake at 350 degrees for 45 minutes or until muffins are brown and crispy around the edges.

## ABOUT THE AUTHOR

Patricia Rockwell is the author of two mystery series. Her Pamela Barnes acoustic mysteries include SOUNDS OF MURDER, FM FOR MURDER, VOICE MAIL MURDER, and STUMP SPEECH MURDER. Her Essie Cobb senior sleuth mysteries include BINGOED, PAPOOSED, and VALENTINED. She is the founder and publisher of Cozy Cat Press, which specializes in producing cozy (or gentle) mysteries.

Patricia has spent most of her life teaching. Her Bachelors' and Masters' degrees are from the University of Nebraska in Speech, and her Ph.D. is from the University of Arizona in Communication. She was on the faculty at the University of Louisiana at Lafayette for thirteen years, retiring in 2007.

Her publications are extensive, with over 20 peer-reviewed articles in scholarly journals, several textbooks, and a research book on her major interest area of sarcasm, published by Edwin Mellen Press. In addition to publications, she served for eight years as editor of the *Louisiana Communication Journal*. Her research focuses primarily on deception, sarcasm, and vocal cues.

Dr. Rockwell is presently living in Aurora, Illinois, with her husband Milt, also a retired educator.

www.ingramcontent.com/pod-product-compliance
Lightning Source LLC
Chambersburg PA
CBHW050420260626
47156CB00003B/1089